crunch

Also by Matt Marshall

The Starlight Line

Friction

crunch

Matt Marshall

CAGED LETTER PRESS

Caged Letter Press

ISBN: 978-0-9972120-3-7

Printed in the United States of America

10 9 8 7 6 5 4 3 2

Cover: Francisco de Goya, *Escapan entre las llamas*, from the series *Desastres de la guerra* (Cleveland Museum of Art).

For the species that follow

At the center, hovering over or perhaps tethering all the rest, is a cloud, painted to puffed, threatening proportions, its gray mass outlined by paint of a dark charcoal hue, rounding wetly to form a very stylized, hard-set depiction of a billowing cumulonimbus. Streaks of orange within the mass of condensed vapor add to the sky's threatening appearance. Directly beneath the cloud, and tied to it by a thick line of black paint, is a female figure in a white lab coat bent over slightly to her right with her shoulders hunched and the fingers of her hands intertwined just below the chin, giving her the air of a vampire or some other dastardly character, albeit one surrounded by golden rays of light. Her unkempt hair swirls about her face, tossed by an apparently strong, wet wind. To her right is a pair of lab technicians, a woman and a man, perhaps colleagues of the woman at the painting's center, likewise tethered to the cloud with a line of black paint and stationed behind a microscope, the man's eyes set to the scope and the woman instructing or clarifying something to him. On the other side of the painting is an old man with a pale face and a large white beard, a farmer or gardener apparently, cutting a row in the soil in front of him with a hoe. To his left and, judging by the proportion, farther back in the scene, is a detective in traditional garb of trench coat and fedora, his hands stuffed into the pockets of his coat, his head down as he walks with an aimless, preoccupied air, though perhaps this is but the practiced nonchalance of a skilled, professional dick hot on the heels of his target, a target that here, based on the positioning of the figures, seems to be the farmer, though the painting, to be sure, is not meant to represent spatial reality. So perhaps the detective is after someone else entirely or, perhaps, he is after no one at all. He tugs his hat down closer to his eyes. Then, or at the same time as he does this, he begins to descend a craggy stairwell that's been carved from stone, the walls reflecting a dark shimmer, glistening from a days-old rain that has failed to dry, black oily streaks cutting down from an unseen height, sticky with hair and grit. Deep, reverberating gulping sounds plunk from the walls or from beneath the stairs, timed to the detective's footfalls and undergirding his shoes' sharp, echoing smacks against the stone. He stumbles now and reaches out his right arm to steady himself, voicing disgust upon touching the slimy wall and quickly wiping the palm of his hand back and forth across his trench coat. Stopped there roughly halfway down the stairwell, the detective raises his chin and gazes toward the obscured ceiling. His left elbow begins to shake noticeably against his ribs, causing the cigarette at the end of his extended forearm to quickly vibrate. He clasps his left wrist with his right hand until the vibrating stops. Then he raises the cigarette to his mouth with extreme deliberateness and inserts the filter between his lips. After puncturing the bundled flesh of the scrotum, the hemostat gathers the vas deferens and tugs it free of the skin till the tube is displayed in a tiny white loop. Two tiny clamps are placed on the loop and a scissors clips twice to the inside of each clamp, causing the looped section to fall away. Each fresh end of the tube is then tied off with stitches and the strands are tucked back inside the punctured scrotum. The second vas deferens is likewise exposed, clamped, cut, tied off, and returned to its sack. The penis, which heretofore had been held up and away against the man's lower belly by a piece of Scotch tape, is released and allowed to fall back over the scrotum. The woman who has just performed the vasectomy places her surgical tools in a small pouch, which she then slips into a pocket on the inside of her jacket near her left breast. She stands and spins away from the man reclined unconscious in the office chair and takes a pen from the desk. She scrawls something on the top leaf of a pad of Easter green Post-it notes. She peels the note loose from the pad, turns back to the man and adheres her message to his pubic hair with the green square draping over the shaft of the penis. That would change everything, he says, fastening the penultimate button at the top of his shirt. The woman he is addressing has bent down to retrieve her bra from the floor and, standing now, slips it on over her breasts and fastens it at her back in one fluid motion. It's just a possibility, she says, don't go picking out names just yet. The corners of her mouth curl down to stifle a grin. The man is not amused. He challenges her for a moment with a hard, granite look, then exhales briskly through his nostrils. Some of us aren't so flippant about these issues, he tells her. No? she replies, and how about the cocks of these serious fellows? Are they concerned? Clearly upset now, the man turns away from her and fishes a sport coat from the back of a chair that has been set at a 45-degree angle from the rectangular mirror that stretches across a large portion of the hotel room's wall. The woman comes up behind him and wraps her arms around his midsection, interlacing her fingers just above his navel. Her chin nestles into the crook of his neck. Her eyes close and the line of her lips softens. The shoulders of the farmer, working under a bright afternoon sun, twist to his right as he brings the hoe up from the dirt, stretches it forward and plants it down again hard into the earth. His elbows bend, biceps flex, as he drags the hoe toward himself, plowing the dirt, then twists his shoulders again to lift the tool and repeat the action. A single bead of sweat runs from beneath his wide-brimmed straw hat and traces a wet line down his left temple, cheek and neck, to be sopped finally by the cotton collar of his yellowed T-shirt. Another stroke of his hoe tills the dry dirt. The rhythmic drop-and-drag of his tool sounds not unlike brushes on a snare drum, a rhythm he begins to moan over presently, humming something with the feel of an old spiritual. And, indeed, the soulful moans soon turn verbal, starting with a very general character—Ohhhh Lorrrrr-orrrd—then, after several more rakings of the earth, singing a more pointed, individualistic tune: Ohhh how I've travelled / Saaaailed my Lorrrd / Caaast off and Ruuuined / Myyy-eye Lord / Taaaken by your waaters / Taaaken from my faamily / Taaaken from my couuntry / Led into Ruuuu-in / But reboorrr-orn / Myyyy Lorrrrd / Reeeeeborrr-horn / Leeeead me onnn Lor-hord / Leeead me ah-honnn. He lets the rubber strap go from his teeth and removes the needle from his left forearm. His eyes close and his head falls back with an alarming looseness, the base of the skull knocking against the stone wall behind his chair and his jaw dropping open. A gurgling noise rises from his throat and bubbles on for an extended period. A broken cackle coughs out from the shadows. That's the fine-grained silt, 'tective, runs the voice that emerges from the laughter. None that *loam* shit! The detective remains motionless, splayed out in his chair against the wall, silent now. Take it easy, de-tec-tive. Don't now slip away from me. And the shadow resumes its cackling. The squatting man rests the rifle against the short concrete wall that rims the top of the building. He slips his right arm free of the backpack strap then frees his left, allowing the pack to slide to the roof's flat concrete surface. A sudden, forceful breeze hits him from the rear, causing him to hunch his shoulders and look up to follow the breeze's path out over the city's buildings, lifting birds here and there, pushing power lines and various other wires and cables, rattling unseen pieces of vinyl siding and metal. The manufacturing of consent, the man mutters, tugging his cap down securely on his head and taking up his gun again, resting its barrel on the roof's wall so that it points out in line with the wind. Thin threads of purplish plastic can be seen here and there just beneath the skin on his forearms, looking like faded streaks of blue or black or red ink, surfacing and falling from the skin in an irregular stitch. His left index finger absently strokes one of these marks on his right forearm, moving over it in a slow, back-and-forth motion. But his gaze remains fixed on the roofs of the hundreds of buildings in front of him or on the sky just above them. The sharp shadow cast beneath the curve of his right cheekbone carves a strong, appealing crag into his cheek. The width of the shadow fluctuates as his jaw tenses and releases in a nervous gnaw he is likely unaware of executing. The dark bending streak grows thin then widens as if seen through rippling water. The line, faint at its head, quickly darkens as it comes down the page and turns sharply to the right. The felt-tipped pen leans a touch, increasing the line's thickness as the side of the pen's tip presses more firmly against the paper, so that the line has tripled or quadrupled in width by the time it hits the second turn and continues straight down the page for a few inches before veering left (and thinning once more) to begin a loop that circles around and closes on the right, forming an expansive teardrop shape. Inside the teardrop the pen now writes the word LAKE in a brittle script. Along the line of the tributary leading down to the lake the pen writes the word RIVER in the same unsteady hand with the initial R lowermost in the progression that runs up the left side of the line, the word's base remaining more or less equidistant from the line while its top slopes down toward the line as it goes, with each letter a touch shorter than the one that precedes it. The difference in height, the consistent stepping down of the heads, as seen from the rear, gives the impression that the row of people is positioned on a staircase that is being rolled along the sidewalk, the people mere passengers. A woman in a rain jacket, her right hand clutched over her left breast, preventing the medical pouch in her pocket from jostling, sweeps out from behind this slow-moving line of progressively smaller people, releasing an exasperated sigh as she hurries past them on their left and continues to snake her way through the throngs crowding the lunch-hour sidewalk, few in the mass moving with any great urgency and many stopped altogether, chatting and laughing in small groups that clog the flow of people, forcing walkers to loop around to the left or the right, a traffic pattern not enforced in any manner so that there is much bunching and jostling for position as the north- and south-going pedestrians try to make their way along the route. The pink fleshy forms stretch and push into one another, appearing as wet flower buds mashing into a flow that swims or sails or rides around islands of clumped blood cells, the moving cells pressed helplessly into spinning and crushing as they slide along, slipping with the stream off the lower-right corner of the frame. The technician lifts his eyes from the scope and blinks several times. He turns to the lead scientist standing next to him and attempts a smile. The scientist lifts her eyebrows slightly and frowns. You see how it is? she says. Yes, he replies, grinning. But no. Her laugh startles the patrons seated in groups of two and three and four at the small round tables outside the café. Ignoring their surprised reactions, or likely not even registering the reactions and perhaps not even the people themselves, she cuts through the tightly configured tables, making her way to one situated on the right corner of the patio, up against the building, where the man in the sport coat sits smiling, watching her approach. You're such a bastard, she calls to him laughingly, drawing yet more turned heads, which she continues to ignore. The man rises halfway from his chair as she reaches the table, then sits again as she sits. Even when I'm on time, I'm late, she tells him, the generally lighthearted expression on her face offset by a pinching of her eyebrows. You should know by now, he says flatly, which she acknowledges with a noncommittal hum, reclining in her chair and turning her head to look back in the direction from which she came. With his eyes barely remaining open, the detective's chin sinks slowly toward his chest then jerks suddenly upward. His eyelids, likewise, begin to lift, but then spasm from the effort and fall closed again. The tires of a red Pontiac Fiero roll slowly over the parking lot of crushed stone, releasing a pleasant crunching sound. The door opens, and the bronzed leg of a teenage girl swings out. When will we go? the smiling girl asks later, her head seeming to float like a balloon above the table, hovering at the top of her neck, a white radiance easing her away from her surroundings. Soon, he says, and feels the vibration in the air. A large stone presses down on everything. His eyes still closed, he takes his head in his hands, elbows on thighs, thumbs pressed to the corners of his jaws, fingers splayed across the frontal dome of his skull. He takes a deep breath, exhales slowly, breathes in again, spits. He jolts back in his chair and his eyes spring open. A groan parts his lips, stretching the corners of his mouth downward as it gains force, exposing a set of clenched teeth that pops open moments later to release the painful scream. A thrust of brackish water pushes over the cement embankment and washes into the grass. A few seconds later, a larger quantity of water jumps the wall and rushes farther into the grass, leaving a yellow-white foam in the crevices between the stiff green blades as the stream of water recedes or soaks into the dirt. The bubbles of the foam crackle and burst in sputtering succession beneath the glare of the late-morning sun. Then the grass is flooded again by a fresh surge of water. The hoe strikes the dirt and rips it back. Tentacles of roots pitch up from the newly dug trench, their thin, white limbs flashing cool in the sunlight. The surrounding dirt is rendered in flat streaks or clumps of gray. An intensely dark, wet speck appears now at a point on the left slope of the trench, its darkness soon swallowed by the dry dirt. Bringing his legs in line with one another and hinging his torso straight upright from the waist, the farmer guides the butt of the hoe to his navel, allowing it to rest there as he reaches into the left back pocket of his overalls and draws forth a faded handkerchief that he uses to swab the sweat from his brow. He exhales audibly, then brings the coffee mug to his lips. His eyes close as he drinks, reopening only after he has drawn the mug away from his mouth again. You *tamed* another one, I take it, he says, returning the mug to the table. The woman grins, bending in to blow over her steaming cup of tea. The service has been rendered, yes, she acknowledges. The voice is gone now from the shadows in front of him, the raspy breathing too. You there, Dirt? the detective asks nonetheless. The pole is planted roughly halfway up the side of the trench. The soldier squats to pack dirt and rocks around the pole's base. He tests it then by gripping the pole and attempting to shake it. Satisfied, he stands again, resting his hands on his hips and looking to the top of the pole where a rather ornate crucifix, one previously confined to indoor service, no doubt, guiding church processions and the like, has been affixed by a bead of crude but strong-looking welding material. Through billowing smoke and passing clouds, the intricate metal latticework on the cross catches and loses glints of sunlight, causing it to sparkle around the more uniformly illuminated Christ figure. A girl of about five or six flips the page in her oversized storybook and immediately begins to read aloud from the new page, following the text with her index finger. Returning his handkerchief to his pocket, the farmer takes a moment to survey his field. The long trench that runs out across the dirt in front of him is matched by similar trenches to his left, each a straight line from one edge to the other of the rectangular dirt field that covers roughly an acre of land. The farmer has dug his rows across the shorter stretch of the rectangle, leaving about two feet between each row. He is not quite a quarter done with his work. He looks to his right, now, to the smooth unworked dirt that awaits him. And where might these have come from? The scientist shakes her head. That's what we need to figure out. The man on the roof removes the clip from his rifle and packs it away in a long, leather case with a strap that he hoists onto his right shoulder as he stands. Then he turns and walks purposefully over to a steel door located in the center of the cement roof. He opens the door, revealing a flight of steps, which he can be heard descending until the door, eased shut by a rusty but still moderately functional hydraulic door closer, clinks into place behind him. His legs visibly unsteady, with feet often planting pigeon-toed beneath him, the detective lurches along the early morning sidewalk, his bloodshot eyes maintaining a nearly unblinking focus, their gaze directed to the concrete roughly a yard in front of his awkwardly moving feet, seeming to will their continuing operation. His line of sight is depicted by a series of dashes that extends from his eyes to the sidewalk, engaging the ground at a 60-degree angle. His hunched-over form, as printed in black, ink-drawn lines on deeply yellowed paper, shows the detective in profile, cloaked in a rumpled trench coat with his hands stuffed deeply into the coat's pockets. If a line were drawn straight down from his eyes to the sidewalk, connecting with the ground at a 90-degree angle and connecting above with the dashed line-of-sight at a 30-degree angle, that vertical line would intersect with the tip of his right shoe, which appears to cap a rather weak right leg—something in the angle of thigh and perfectly vertical lower leg makes the foundation seem so unsound that it might soon snap at the knee—that, when considered along with the placement of the left shoe, drawn at the end of a seemingly overextended left leg so that the toes alone of the foot are touching the ground, the shoe bending up from the ball of the foot at a 45-degree angle and the ankle jutting back toward the knee at a right angle, approximately, gives the impression of either anatomical inaccuracy or simply a misrepresentation of the human gait, although this impression may derive from the fact that the left leg is covered, from the shin up, by the detective's coat, as are the man's hips, masking what might otherwise strike the viewer as a completely normal human form depicted in midstride. He rides the ocean's wave, his body draped over the truck tire with his forearms gripping the tread, his upper arms and right cheek pressed to the sidewall, his chest and stomach stretched across the rim, his thighs riding the sidewall and his legs, from the knees down, floating in the water behind him. Thus affixed to the tire, riding up and down with the waves, he looks like a strange sea creature: the rubber ring a large, black belly, his dangling legs a forked tail. He lifts and turns his head so that his chin is now resting on the sidewall, his eyes peering blankly, half dead, out into the seemingly endless—and endlessly shifting—peaks and valleys of the sea. The water is painted a bright, royal blue and is shown spilling over a cliff's craggy rock formation a bit north and right of the canvas's center. Protruding from the cliff, and poking through the waterfall, is a bundle of six electrical wires, each so enlarged as to appear to have a diameter of three or four feet when considered in proportion to the waterfall, and each encased in a uniquely colored plastic sheath—red, yellow, green, blue, black, white—that has been stripped near the wire's end, exposing the number of tightly packed copper threads and allowing them to splay at the wire's tip. Lush, green tropical plants grow on either side of the waterfall, covering the full length of the cliff. The greenery becomes less dense the farther one gets from the water, and there, at the edges of their growth, the plants sprout not from the expected rock face but, rather, from walls of electronic equipment. A similar, though much compressed waterfall scene appears in the lower left corner of the canvas. Likewise, the bottom of a falls can be seen dropping from the top of the canvas in the middle of the left side. The left edge of another falls, with surrounding plant life extending to the left, is situated at the right edge of the canvas. The image of a man in a dark gray business suit, white shirt and red tie has been placed over top of the greenery on the left side of the canvas. He is shown in a walking motion, heading toward the left edge of the canvas, his body—extending from mahogany-colored wingtips to short, dark hair, parted on the left—covering roughly two-thirds of the canvas's height. The figure is shifted toward the top of the canvas so that if a centerline were drawn, left to right, it would dissect the man's thighs. His right arm is raised and bent at the elbow, angling the forearm out in front of his chest. A wristwatch is exposed just beyond the cuff of his shirt, and the man is looking down to check the time. His left arm drops straight down the side of his body with the hand gripping a briefcase. A nearly identical man, wearing the same gray suit, but with a blue tie, appears in the lower half of the canvas's right side. He, likewise, is shown walking to the left, his legs and arms positioned exactly like the other man's. He is much smaller than his twin, however, with his entire body fitting easily within the lower-right quadrant of the painting. He too carries a briefcase (apparently of the same make as the other man's) in his left hand, but in his right he holds a smartphone, and there is no watch on his wrist. His head is positioned in the same downward slant as the other man's, and the phone is angled so as to be in his line of sight. In various locations across the expanse of the painting, depictions of rust spots, large and small, appear, giving the impression that the entire tableau is rendered on a large sheet of metal that has begun to deteriorate. This is the Lord's work, the farmer muses, wiping his brow with his handkerchief. I plant the seeds that will sprout a revolution. I need to get back to the office, the man at the café table says. The woman with him hums into the teacup at her lips, then nods several times as she lowers the cup to the table. I have work to get to too, she says. I'll see you later? What is a re-vol-u-tion? the girl asks. The boy sitting next to her doesn't respond, nor does he seem even to have heard the girl's question, his focus remaining fixed on the comic book he is reading. The girl reaches over with her right hand and jostles his left shoulder. Hey! He shrugs it off, still without diverting his attention from the comic book, as if he were absently flinching in reaction to a bothersome fly. What is a rev-lu-tion? she whines, jostling him further. Stop! What *iiiiis* it? A what? he asks, continuing to read. The girl looks back to her book, returning her right index finger to the page to hunt for the unfamiliar word. Re-vol-u-tion. She turns back to the boy who continues to read. She remains silent, watching him, a look of sadness and desperation forming on her face as the boy goes on ignoring her. But then, without warning and still without directing his eyes away from his comic book, he tells her, It's like a battle. The girl returns to her book and rereads the sentence with the unfamiliar word in it, her lips forming the words silently, her eyes and nose scrunching together in continued confusion. She mouths the words again, registering neither comprehension nor befuddlement this time, but simply staring at the page blankly until her attention is diverted by a man passing by her suddenly on the left. I'll call you later, he says. Upon waking, his eyes are aimed directly at his exposed groin, pants and underwear bundled at his ankles, a strange green square affixed to his penis. He sits slouched in the office chair, staring blankly at his lap for several seconds, his arms hanging straight down at his sides, his fingers less than a foot above the floor. Now he jolts upward and looks hurriedly to his left and right, his face distorted by panic. He bends forward and attempts to pull his pants back on, but they become tangled with his underwear in the struggle. He tugs at the pants more forcefully, causing the waistband to get caught up with the seat of the chair, which he is unable to lift himself from sufficiently. He relaxes, then tugs again, still without success. Frustrated, he lets go of the pants, allowing them to fall back to his ankles. He reclines in the chair, resting the top of his head against the chairback with the chin pointing up toward the ceiling. His briefs remain stuck, twisted at his knees. He squeezes his eyes shut for several seconds then opens them again, exhales and sits up in the chair, seemingly more relaxed than before. He lifts his right hand and removes the green Post-it note from his crotch. He turns the note about so he can read the phrase written upon it. We knew this day would come, of course, the scientist says. The technician nods, his eyebrows raised. But we didn't really expect it, he says. *No! Never! Really!* He looks at the note for a few seconds longer, his lips pursed, head shaking slowly back and forth. Then he crumples the note and tosses it into the wastebasket. He pulls his pants on and buckles his belt. The discovery of Kulindadromeus, a small plant-eating dinosaur with feathers and scales, fossils of which were found on the banks of the Olov River in Siberia in 2010, and reported on in 2014, suggested that feathers were much more common in dinosaurs than previously thought. Before this find, only meat-eating dinosaurs had been known to possess feathers. The detective takes a seat outside the café. He pulls a pack of cigarettes from his coat pocket, but stops the motion suddenly—the pack held for a second at chest level—before stuffing the cigarettes back in his pocket. His lips curl under, head tilts. Coffee? asks the waitress who has appeared next to his table. She wears a small white waist apron over her otherwise black attire, accentuating the attractive curve of her abdomen. The detective nods. The sergeant crosses himself. Then, with the same right hand, he lifts the sandwich from his lap and takes a large bite from it. He leans back against the dirt wall of the trench and raises his left hand, turning it about to casually inspect its blackened skin. With his thumbnail he begins to pick away at the dirt lodged beneath the nails of his fingers. He lifts the sandwich again and takes another bite, continuing to pick at his fingernails as he chews. I'm missing you, he says into his phone as he moves up the sidewalk, dodging other pedestrians with the nonchalance of an experienced slalom skier. No, it's not that, he says. After a pause of several seconds, he adds, It's always *you* who's joking. He smiles into the phone, listening and walking quickly up the sidewalk. I think I'm more serious with you, troubled even, and yet happier. Why is that? Christ knows, the farmer says. Before him stands a young immigrant woman, perhaps not even eighteen yet, slight of stature and clothed in a drab pairing of coffee-colored blouse and teal-gray slacks, with blue plastic slip-on shoes. Her long black hair is pulled back in a ponytail that is held by a faded red elastic band that has been twisted several times about itself. The woman lowers her chin after the farmer speaks and does not look at him. Christ knows, he continues, of that you can be sure. Sin does not escape his gaze. The woman mumbles something or, perhaps, she has merely cleared her throat. The farmer tilts his head as he looks at her. I hope you are not thinking of compounding your sin, he says. The girl lifts her head now and sits back in her chair. She pushes her oversized picture book, opened roughly to the midway point, away from her so that it rests squarely on the round café table. She spies the man in the trench coat who lounges in rough, rumpled fashion two tables away from her reading the newspaper. She lifts her hands to her eyes, the fingers forming tubes through which she can better inspect his person. **Refu** seen through the left tube, the letters underlined by the man's knotted right index finger, **cked** seen through the right tube, the letters running into the crevice between the index and middle fingers of the man's left hand. The girl, her lips moving silently, reads the left word and then the right, leaving a gap between the two that decreases as she continues to read them until the two words finally become one, which the girl repeats aloud. The older boy at her table turns away from his comic book, his face evidencing, first, troubled surprise and then, almost immediately after, curious mirth colored by more than a hint of pride. What did you say? Refucked? she repeats, which causes the boy to burst into peals of laughter and the man to lower his paper slightly and, with a flat, tired expression, look at the boy over the top of his reading glasses. He winces now as the boy's laughter spikes anew, and the newspaper begins to rustle in his suddenly shaking hands. The rustling sound draws the girl's head back around where her eyes flash, catching again the headline she had read earlier, this time without the obstruction of her hands. **Refugees Blocked**, she reads, first silently, then, after turning to the boy, aloud and with confidence. Refugees blocked, she repeats in a taunting manner. Refucked, he says, shaking his head and laughing again. The man smiles sleepily and returns to his reading. The sergeant stands and brushes the palms of his hands together to spank off any crumbs left from the sandwich. He sticks a hand up under his cap and scratches his scalp. What news? he asks the teenage boy who stands before him saluting. We've spotted a new raft about two miles out, the boy says, lowering his hand. How full? About fifty to seventy-five of 'em, sir. Arrival? Not before 16:00. The sergeant nods. Prepare the usual welcoming party, he says. We'll hit 'em a mile out. God willing, none of those bastards will ever reach the shore. The boy nods. Nice, he says, flipping the page of his comic book. The barrel of the detective's gun is evidenced by three-quarters of a white circle that peers out from the room's ink blackness like a second right eye that sits just below the white triangle of the detective's right cheekbone. BLAAAAM! Then complete darkness.

The paper target zips into the booth and the shooter inspects his work. His thumb circles over the grouping of shots lodged at the heart of the figure outlined on the target. The thumb circles slowly as in a caress. The hand grips the target and rips it free from its clip. The scientist sits at the desk in her office poring over sheets of paper that are stacked and compartmentalized in several manila folders. The window behind her is black, and a harsh light shines onto her papers from a gooseneck desk lamp. **Manufactured Evolution: The Potential Rise of Generative Molecular-Mechanical Organisms (GMMOs).** The scientist's left hand comes to her forehead as she reads, the fingertips alone pressing against her skull, so that the fingers bend back and up to the bulk of the hand, the whole appearing as some multilegged, parasitic creature latched onto and massaging the scientist's scalp. A gurgling sound can be heard from the gutter, bubbling and burping through the thick metal grating. A spray of spit shoots past the rusted bars. Soon, streams of blackish water are flowing out from the sewer, breaking around the steel bars and reconverging in the street to form one slick, moving entity alive with the mirrored colors of life. Your body does not belong to you, child. Christ paid the ultimate price for it. So use your body to give the proper glory to he who owns it—the Lord, your god. Having said this, the farmer hands the young woman his hoe. The work is before you, he says, his left arm sweeping out over the field in which they are standing. The woman puts her hand, hesitantly, on the tool's wooden handle. She looks meekly at the farmer, who offers her a weak smile before striding off, leaving her with the hoe. She removes the pouch from her jacket and places it on the counter. She takes off her jacket and hangs it on the back of one of the chairs stationed around the kitchen table then returns to the pouch on the counter. She unzips the pouch and removes the surgical instruments. After taking a bottle of isopropyl alcohol from its place there on the counter, along with a cotton ball, removed from a glass jar, she proceeds to unscrew the cap on the bottle, stop the opening with the cotton ball, and tip the bottle to pour a touch of the alcohol into the cotton. She quickly swabs each instrument with the cotton ball, rinses the instrument under the kitchen faucet then sets it in the drying rack in the other side of the sink. Among those stopped at the border were a man, believed to be an ex-doctor, who was carrying surgical instruments and other medical supplies, a man and a woman with possible links to the solar panel industry, and several suspected Muslims. It was not clear how many were in this last group, nor whether they were from the same family or different ones. Officials said twenty-six people in all were stopped, and that most were simply turned away, while some others were held for questioning. They did not indicate how many were held, nor if they were still being detained or had subsequently been released. She lays the dried instruments out on a double layer of blue CSR paper. She opens each instrument—the two hemostats and the scissors—as wide as it will go and places a cotton ball in the bottom of the hinge to prevent the instrument from closing. She stacks the instruments neatly in a line, one above the other but with considerable overlap, and lays an autoclave indicator strip on top of the pile. She folds up the bottom edge of the innermost sheet of CSR paper, making the flap large enough so that she can also fold it back on itself halfway. Then she folds in the lower right corner, followed by the entire right side of the sheet, folding the excess back and forth on top of the instruments in paper fan style to create a snug wrapping. She folds in the lower left corner and left side in the same manner as the right then folds the top of the paper down. She folds the outer sheet of paper in a manner similar to the first and, when finished, rips off two strips of autoclave tape from a roll on the counter and wraps each around the blue package to hold it closed. She places the package on a tray in the small autoclave that sits on the kitchen counter, closes the door and turns the lock until it's tight. She adjusts the time and temperature dials, sets the autoclave to sterilize, then turns the machine on. Leaving the newspaper offices, the journalist hurries up the street and hops onto a small pesero bus that has just swooped in toward the curb and is now leaving again, the action between man and bus performed as an expertly timed, choreographed routine. After paying his fare, the journalist maneuvers his way past a few people standing in the aisle and takes up a space near the back of the bus. Six or seven blocks down the street he presses the button on the pole next to the exit door and descends the steps as the door opens and the pesero swings in again toward the curb. Gracias! he calls, stepping out. Seconds later he is set upon by a man in a dirty black trench coat who escapes from the sidewalk's bustle, draws forth a rusty machete and brings it down in two quick, successive chops to the back of the journalist's neck. The assassin gone, the journalist's butchered body lies alone on the cement, pushing away spectators with a neat, circumferential force. Far beneath the body, layered sheets of clay and volcanic soil break down and collapse, sending seismic ripples upwards. Bills are slipped out from a leather wallet and placed on the glass counter. The detective lights a cigarette. He drinks his coffee. He considers with a scowl the crowd assembled on the patio around him. The fingers of his left hand tap nervously against the tabletop. He smokes, and drinks his coffee. At the base of a nearby table a black dog sniffs for scraps, licking the ground frequently to sample the invisible sources of various scents. His nose pokes into one of the wedges at the table's base where it splits into the cross of its four supporting beams. Tail wagging furiously, the dog continues to sniff about, working his way across one of the supporting horizontal legs, then, having discovered nothing of substance to keep him there, tracing a scent that leads from the table leg, across the cement, to a leg on the detective's table, along the edge of it, up the center-leg support, stopping about halfway up and sniffing intently and licking, sniffing and licking, then down again to the ground and picking up the scent on the leg perpendicular to that which brought him into the table and out the length of this leg, discovering nothing, then out across the cement again to the badly scuffed, scent-laden toe leather on the right foot of the rumpled gumshoe. The detective reaches down and scratches the dog between the ears. The dog looks up and licks the man's knee. So what I'm proposing is that we sneak away somewhere—somewhere quiet where we can get better acquainted. You're joking, the man in suit and tie insists. Not at all, the woman says. Well, this is all very unexpected, he laughs nervously. I really don't know how I could swing it. So, that's a no, then? He remains silent. I asked you a question! the man in the black uniform thunders. A streak of blue light reflects off the dome of his shaved head. No, you're not a citizen? No, I no have ID, the other man, dressed in a sand-colored windbreaker, responds. You no have ID, the man in black nods, appearing tired and annoyed. A grin curves his lips and he makes a display of chomping his gum. No ID is bad, he tells the other man. You understand? Bad. I no have, the other man says. I know you no have. You no have shit. And that's bad, you understand? That's bad for you. The other man doesn't say anything. What can I do? he asks then. Hmmm, I wonder. The man shrugs. Think, she says, impatiently. He gives her an embarrassed grin, followed by a nervous laugh. She raises her eyebrows, insisting. Nowhere? I don't know, he begins. Nowhere? I don't … No place that you have all to yourself, with a door that closes and locks, and where no one will bother us? He stops smiling and looks at her more intently, his face showing a sign of recognition. The office? he asks. They continue looking at one another for a time, uncomfortable grins mirrored on their faces. Bingo, she says, finally, poking him in the chest with an index finger. The large tire brushes across the sand, pushed up the beach by the incoming tide and producing a harsh, ripping noise as the rubber scrapes over the sheet of packed silt. The tire slides just beyond the tidemark and appears to slip back a bit toward the ocean as the wave is pulled back that way, but perhaps that slip is just an optical illusion. The white, starfish-like form draped over the tire's center, its body blanched by the sun or film of salt, slowly reveals itself as the body of a man. The straggly mop of gray hair at the top and the bolt of faded blue cloth belted about the midsection—apparently the shredded remains of a pair of pants—eventually bring this conclusion into focus. For a long time the man lies stretched upon the tire unmoving, his white skin reflecting a piercing signal in the afternoon sun. Then his shoulders lift, one before the other, an initial movement recognized, perhaps, only in relation to the subsequent, more-pronounced arm movements—a trick of memory to re-create the missed action that must have preceded that which was knowingly seen. The whole body stirs then, a quick sequence of motion that escapes easy dissection— what happened first?—more an involuntary ripple of muscle than a directed effort. Still, it has the effect of tipping the man off the tire and into an awkward, uncomfortable-looking pile on the sand. The black dog sits next to the detective's knee, his wet chestnut eyes casually inspecting the comings and goings on the café patio and the sidewalk and street beyond. When something catches his attention, the muscle above one eye or the other rises and expands, rippling the velvet skin. A revolver is pressed to the man's temple and the trigger is pulled. Done. We're just getting started the woman purrs into his ear. She lowers her head a touch and licks the man's neck. Her left hand caresses the front of his chinos, massaging the mass behind the zipper with increasing urgency. Hmmm, shall we have a look? She positions the slide on the microscope and puts her eyes to the eyepieces. The fingers of her left hand play at the adjustment knob, mimicking the knitting legs of a spider. The corners of her lips expand and relax as she continues to view the sample under the microscope. Occasionally she makes a low, guttural noise. Insane, she whispers, admiring the engorged glans. She covers it with her mouth then slowly pulls back, the tip of her tongue licking the underside as she releases fully from his member. She looks up at the man briefly then puts the erect penis back in her mouth, guiding it with her left hand, which completely surrounds the shaft. She slides her lips down to meet the ring of forefinger and thumb then comes back up, pausing for a moment at the rim of the glans before moving down again. Soon she has fallen into a relaxed, rhythmic pumping motion: the blade of the hoe hits the dirt and is drawn back, hits the dirt and is drawn back. Pebbles fall beyond the returning blade, tumbling with small clumps of dirt to line the bottom of the freshly hewn trough. Occasionally the woman scrapes the trough to clear it of the fallen debris. But as she continues in her work, moving backwards toward the edge of the field, she becomes less vigilant about removing the pebbles, raking each spot once or twice before taking a few steps back and attacking new ground. Rocks and dirt shower down. A high-frequency whine follows, cutting sharply into the air over the field. Or maybe the noise had always been there but has just now become heightened for some reason. The piercing noise continues as a crossweave of sonic movement, layering and layering, gaining in volume and testing the greater reaches of sound. A line dips. The noise of accelerated falling. A quick black brushstroke across an unstable, watery sky. Bangs into the earth just above the trench, exploding in a flash of light so intense as to seem beyond light, a blast of sound so great as to escape sound. And the dirt and smoke rain down on the soldiers huddled under ponchos in the trench. The sergeant stands while much of the dust from the explosion is still rising. He yells into the air's deafening scream, the contortions of his face revealing the frustration of trying to shout down the commotion. His arms flail, then lock into more regimented motion, with the left forearm pivoting forcefully back and forth from the elbow, the forefinger extended, and the right forearm twirling at the elbow, the hand waving his men forward. The high-frequency whine blasts into silence. Done. The detective's eyes relax noticeably and he exhales. There, he sighs, the silt has settled. He scratches the dog between the ears. When will we go? the girl asks. Her toes dig out a corkscrew pattern in the dark, packed sand. Later, perhaps immediately after she completes the design, seawater rushes in, causing her to squeal and throw her feet into the air as the flood erases her work and soaks again the bottom half of her bikini. She sits next to the window knitting a yet unidentifiable creation from multicolored yarn as the bus moves by fits and starts along the city street. Occasionally, especially when the bus jolts to a stop, she looks up and out the window, her brow pinching together in surprise or annoyance. But her hands do not falter, continuing to stitch away with their needles, demonstrating the divergent paths of action between hands and eyes, which heretofore had seemed necessarily interlinked—one guiding the other—but now appear wholly unrelated; correlation instead of causation. Still, as the bus drifts back into traffic, the eyes cast downward again and take up their vigil as before. The detective lifts the coffee mug and drinks from it, noticing, as he moves to place the mug down again, the crude circle of perspiration that has been left on the tabletop. He sets the mug to the side of the moisture. Then with his index finger he draws a spiral design in the film of humidity, starting at the center and looping up and around it once, then twice, and lifting his finger from a point more or less straight down from where he had started drawing. She descends again, her eyes cast upwards to see the effect she is having on the man. From a position of burgeoning ecstasy, his head tilted back against the top of his chair, lips parted, his chin drops suddenly onto his chest, his head rolling slightly to the right. The woman stops her motion with fully half of the erect penis still in her mouth. She studies the man's face, his breathing, his general liveliness. After several seconds, she lifts her mouth off the member and lets go the grip of her left hand. With her right, she removes the tranquilizing needle from the man's inner right thigh and returns it to the pocket in her jacket, from which she then draws a faux leather pouch. She lifts the pouch's flap and takes out a package wrapped in blue paper. She lays it on the desk and rips off the tape holding it together. Then she opens the paper, revealing the surgical instruments held within. The gaunt, bearded man sits cross-legged on the beach striking two small stones together over a collection of twigs and branches. After a long series of failed attempts, a decent spark is finally struck, catching a dead leaf in the pile and pulling from it a long, upward-drifting puff of smoke that goes, and is gone, leaving the pile of debris as before, dormant. Only later, after fifteen seconds or so, can an orange glow be seen at the heart of the pile, slowly, steadily gaining force. The wood begins to crackle. A line is cast, a reassuring whiz across the early morning air, then a plop and echoing rings on the water. Gears of the fishing rod whirl a quiet, liquid sound. Then rest. The bus slows and the woman stuffs her knitting into her bag. She rises from her seat, lifting the strap of her bag onto her right shoulder then grabbing hold of the post by the bus's back door. When the bus stops and the door opens, the woman descends onto the sidewalk and walks off to the left with the practiced, unhesitating motion of one who knows where she's going. A brown insect crawls up over the curb, scurries along it, then swoops down to the road, disappearing into the sewer grate. Water rushes from the end of the yellow hose connected twenty yards back to the pump where the road has flooded. The machete hacks into fresh meat. We won't go, will we? she asks. Of course we'll go, he says. When? We'll go, he says. She frowns slightly, not saying anything for several moments, but continues to look at him sadly, disappointed, frustrated. Can I ask you something? she says, finally. With the penis now limp, the saggy skin of the scrotum is punctured, the white cord is drawn out, clamped and snipped. The bearded man wakes by the smoldering embers of the fire he had struck sometime earlier. He sits up and looks out at the ocean. Then he bows his head and mumbles a stream of words, a prayer seemingly. He lifts his head and crosses himself. That's when I found him, he tells the young female farmhand who has just finished hoeing a row in the dirt and stands now in the grass at the edge of the field, the back of her right hand pressed against her forehead. There, on that beach, he says. When I had nothing. I opened and let him in. The woman removes the hand from her head and nods slowly. From the bus stop she moves quickly along the sidewalk, threading her way between slower-going pedestrians. After a block and a half she turns suddenly and enters a tall office building with a height of twenty stories or so. The revolving door turns heavily to a stop after she enters. The line reels in slowly, leaving two rippling lines in its wake. With both tied-off cords returned to their pouch, a Band-Aid is placed over the tiny puncture wound. The woman packs up her instruments, then takes a black Sharpie from her pocket and scrawls three words on the man's abdomen: *No! Never! Really!* She recaps the marker, stands, and, after observing the unconscious man for a few seconds, turns and leaves the office. The hard-set jaw of the sergeant seems to tremble from the force of the awful barrage, his open eyes quake and glisten with a film of moisture. His lips part over clenched teeth as if he might speak. But he says nothing. He stares hard, his eyes narrowing. Then he lifts himself from his chair at the café table. He gives the dog at his feet a final scratch between the ears, stuffs his folded newspaper between his body and left arm and walks away from the table. The boy with the comic book looks up and nods. Entering the office, the woman is met by a massive desk that stretches nearly wall to wall in the oblong reception area. Behind it is stationed a young woman, rather heavily made-up, with straight dark hair that falls to just above her shoulders. She smiles with excessive sweetness at the woman who has entered the office and asks how she can be of assistance. The woman gives the name of the man she is there to see. The receptionist nods and says, I'll tell him you're here. Please have a seat. The woman does so, selecting from a line of stout, wooden chairs with firmly padded, burgundy-clothed seats the one placed closest to the round, two-tiered wooden table in the corner loaded with magazines. She picks from the collection an economic publication with the cover story "Will Declining Birthrates Wreck Your Retirement?" and begins to leaf through it. Through the lens of the scope, the dark figure looks at once very close and very far away, silently gesticulating as it moves through its hazy environment, appendages appearing to form, extend and melt away again as the figure moves along from right to left. It jerks suddenly, then falls in a heap, and the scene as a whole is swept suddenly downward and to the right where it disappears altogether, replaced by a cityscape as viewed from the top of a ten-story building. The man kneeling there stands his rifle on its butt as he drags a large duffel bag to him, opens it and stuffs the gun inside. He zips the bag and hoists its strap onto his right shoulder as he stands. Moving quickly, though not running, he follows a direct line to the metal door located at the roof's center. He swings the door open and skips down the steps within. Is it traceable? The scientist shakes her head, then immediately shrugs her shoulders. Who knows, she says. It's very unlikely, though, that these organisms, nanobots, whatever you want to call them, aren't more widespread than this. We couldn't have just happened upon the one and only subject. Her inquisitor frowns, shuffles through some papers placed before him on the meeting room table. I assume I don't need to tell you, he says, looking up from the papers, none of which apparently contained the information he was seeking, that this all needs to be kept very quiet. The skies opened up then above that beach, creating a deep black gouge in the bluish-gray dawn. Lines of clouds billowed away from this ominous and expanding blackness like lips furrowing over a gaping mouth that seemed ready to swallow me and the rest of the world into its limitless depth. Everything got very cold and still. And he spoke. In an all-consuming voice that issued no words, nor sounds of any kind, but came round me like a hand and held me in its grip, instilling its message through a warm, damning pressure. And my purpose was instantly known to me. To ascribe words to that message would fail to convey all that it was. Suffice it to say that when I stood up again on that beach, after the mouth of the universe had closed above me and been sealed over by the wet, gray morning, I was the man you see before you now. A prophet, some call me, and perhaps that is the best word, although it reeks of too much self-importance for my taste. I am but a vessel—a tool, like that hoe that I have given you to till the earth—through which the Supreme Being might make himself known to his creation and might plant visions of the creation's tangling brilliance. The farmer pauses then, the fingers of his left hand beginning to play absently with the strands of beard situated immediately beneath his lower lip. An impish grin curls his mouth. No, he says to his young acolyte, I don't know exactly what that means, either. The sidewalk goes milky, flowing in soft, comforting waves of motion, carrying the detective forward. He ceases to walk. The air warms and cradles his skull in its tender hands. He floats. He puts his hands in the pockets of his trench coat, his right encountering a sculpture of metal with which his fingers freely commune, one lacing into the form's single opening, the others folding around its thick handle. He holds it. The sidewalk carries him along. The taut line reels in, leaving two undulating streaks in its wake. Quiet. Men of various ages, from those in their early twenties to those nearing retirement, bustle by on the sidewalk, cloaked in gray or khaki slacks, short-sleeved polos or pressed, long-sleeved dress shirts, half-ankle boots or oxfords, most carrying large paper cups filled with coffee and topped with plastic caps, evidencing worry or laughter, walking, pushing past the others on the sidewalk or laying back, loping along in broad, chit-chatting lines of three or four. He'll see you now, the receptionist says. Sitting at a neatly ordered desk in a brightly lit office, the door closed, the man recently returned from the café stares off toward the ceiling, ignoring the computer monitor set before him on the desk. He hums vaguely and occasionally shakes his head. After several minutes he looks suddenly to the monitor and his fingers light upon the keyboard, tapping away in a flurry. He types steadily for close to thirty seconds, pauses to read what he has written, then begins to type again, pauses, reads, types, and continues this routine through several more cycles before finally sitting back in his chair and staring at the screen. He rubs the top of his head with his left hand, exhales, then sits up and strikes a final key. So how am I doing? she asks after settling into the chair on the other side of the financial advisor's desk. He sounds a laugh, then responds in a soft, reassuring voice, leaning in over the desk, his hands stacked upon a manila folder lightly filled with papers, Fine, just fine. But, he says, sitting back suddenly and turning to the computer monitor set off at an angle in the corner of the L-shaped desk, we could always be doing better, yes? She shakes her head. I don't know. Well, let's take a look, he offers, beginning to tap at his keyboard. **WARNING:**

CONSUMING SEAFOOD MAY EXPOSE YOU TO DIOXINS, PCBs, MERCURY AND PLASTIC CONTAMINANTS. You're currently at 80,000, he says flatly. He taps again at his keyboard, observes the current window for a few seconds, then clicks into a new one and types some more. Yes, he says after reading through some material displayed on the screen, 80,000. He turns back to her with an inquisitive look on his face, fishing for some comment—some instruction—from her before proceeding with the investigation into her affairs. She laughs. So it's still hopeless, she jokes. I'll be in debt for the rest of my days. No, no, he assures her, turning his body fully away from the computer and resting his hands again on top of the manila folder. We can devise a more aggressive plan, if you want. But the best, perhaps, is not to dwell on it too much. Let the payments happen. You'll get there before you know it. He attempts a reassuring grin, but it never forms convincingly, and soon his lips have collapsed into a hard-edged, impatient frown. I'm screwed, she says, let's admit it. All I'm working for is food, rent and this loan. I can barely afford yarn, she says, sticking her hand into her bag and lifting her knitting partway from it. The financial advisor stretches the frown on his face and nods in a show of compassion. It's not uncommon, he says after a while. But, still, you'd wish the men would show a little more spunk. We barely held ourselves together today. They could have totally buried us. The lieutenant grimaces and nods. It's nothing new, he tells the sergeant, his voice conveying both wisdom and weariness, dipping toward the latter as he continues. It can help at times to surrender to notions of destiny—God and country and all that. If the Lord is with us who can be against us. All that shit. I don't think the infidels have got the message, the sergeant jokes. They seem to think that God is on *their* side. A notion we need to bomb out of them, the lieutenant pronounces in a rough-edged manner that cuts between a grunt and a laugh. The water runs along the curb in a smooth, flowing sheet, carrying the occasional stick or leaf that shows just how rapidly the water is moving, a speed difficult to discern from watching the flow of water alone. A mosquito lights upon the stream and is immediately sent into a swirl as the water pushes it down the street and out of sight. Watching for even a few minutes allows one to see just how quickly the water is flooding the street. It is almost to the top of the curb now. A large twig comes racing into view, riding the water in a partially upright manner with its top leaning back so that parts of the twig's four or five leaves drag in the water, creating thin green reflections that streak behind it. The twig stops now and stands up straight with its leaves held completely aloft above the water's force, the twig snagged apparently in the sewer grate, a pronounced ripple created on either side of the wood, the water twirling in tightly spun lines of minuscule reflections like braids of exquisitely chiseled crystal. Watching them, it becomes difficult to discern if the ripples are continuing to move or have not, rather, entered some odd physical realm that allows them to remain stationary on the water's surface. What does it take to go forward? he wonders aloud, his features twisted by surprise, whether from having spoken when he had not intended to or from some unspoken answer that has come to him that he had not foreseen. Whatever the case, he now looks more troubled than surprised as he sits with his back pressed up against the trench, the fingers of his left hand absently picking at a scab of dried dirt on the knee of this left pants leg, which, like the right, is bent up sharply to his chest so that the soles of his boots press into the trench's muddy floor, holding him in place against the wall. **Men mysteriously sterilized. Victims of unwanted vasectomies report being seduced, drugged.** It's my worst fear realized, one victim said. Many of the men also complained of being robbed while unconscious. The detective folds his paper and stuffs it into an outer pocket of his trench coat. He takes a final drag from his cigarette, flicks the butt to the sidewalk and grinds it out with the toe of his shoe. He adjusts the brim of his hat then moves on. Standing in line for the bank tellers, a line designated by heavy velvet ropes, mauve and drooping, strung between waist-high copper poles placed three or four feet apart, the woman looks absently at the large painting hung on the wall directly across from the tellers. At the painting's center is a waterfall, intensely blue in color, surrounded by green foliage.

Large electrical wires—red, yellow, green, blue, black, white—protrude from the top of the falls, which appears to be rushing over a wall of electronic equipment, possibly a giant computer server. In various spots across the painting (and in various sizes) are images of a businessman walking to the left, each man holding a briefcase in his left hand, and either looking at a watch strapped to his right wrist or at a smartphone held in his right hand. Rust appears to corrode the painting in several spots. The woman who had recently performed the vasectomy on the unsuspecting man draped helplessly in his office chair, inches forward with the line leading to the tellers, continuing to look at the painting. The golden statue of an angel, her chin held high, chest thrust forward, right arm extended and holding a laurel wreath, balancing (almost floating) on a planted right leg with the left kicked up and back, wobbles now atop her pedestal. Office towers nearby can be seen shaking as well, vibrating in the hot afternoon, sprinkling shards of glass, metal and plastic onto the pavement below. Hanging planters sway heavily within an office. Stacks of papers plummet from their perches atop filing cabinets as inhabitants of the blue, low-definition space hustle for the exits. There is no going back once we start, the farmer intones. Under a hard-set brow he scans the twenty or so field hands gathered before him in the large, open space of the barn. Behind the farmer, bright bars of light cut through the gaps separating the barn's long wooden planks, casting strong backlighting and making it difficult to see the farmer's features as he speaks. The Lord calls and we go. The floodwaters are tears for his creation. They wash us free from the sticky pores of sin where we'd sought easy, moneyed comfort and send us out to sink or swim, to lodge ourselves once again in the thick mud of pleasure and pride or to rise above and do the hard work of cultivating the earth for his glory. One path leads to swinish joy and eternal death, the other to righteous suffering and eternal life. Choose now, then don't turn back. I dare say the Lord favors more those who honestly choose the life of sin and debauchery than those we take up the cross only to buckle under its weight and scurry away into the mud. Know thy burden before ye accept the yoke. The farmer pauses again and makes a stronger sign of inspecting his charges, shifting his feet to turn his entire body, first to the right then scanning back to the left. We will plow, he says, almost inaudibly. Then he repeats it more forcefully, his chin lifting with his voice. We will plow! Sweeping in for closer inspection, the terrible emotion can be seen in the farmer's face, his bottom lip trembling, his eyes brimming with tears. A stack of ten- and twenty-dollar bills is laid on the faux marble counter, a deposit slip placed atop the stack. More *donations* to the women's health fund? the teller asks as she retrieves the stack of bills, a mischievous grin and raised eyebrow betraying some secret, some shared understanding, between the two. The woman nods, her own lips evidencing a tired, rather forced (and failing) attempt at a smile. What can I do? I'm going underground, Dirt, the detective, now in deep shadow, announces, his hands stuffed deeply into the pockets of his raincoat, his shoulders hunched forward, his chin held close to his chest, the brim of his hat pulled down to shadow his eyes. I'm gonna need a supply. Immediately the dry cackle. That'll cost ya, de-tec-tive. Then a full-throated laugh, blowing out in loud, clipped bursts, like an over-choked tractor motor. You got the doouugh? Heh? Heh? Heh? We could maybe work something out? the detective suggests. Wh-? Wha-? What was that, captain? The faceless voice suddenly projecting a serious tone with a threatening hint of violence. That sounds an awful lot like no money to me, tec-tive. Nowwwww, the laugh returning, surely it ain't like that, is it detective? The chin rises from the chest, catching an orange light. You're dirty slime, the detective says flatly. Ah, ain't that the truth, ain't that the truth, the darkness confirms warmly. The world's a dirty place, ah boy ... A block of silence follows during which the lines of shadow outlining the hunched detective and the protrusions of brick in the wall behind him remain completely still, the soundtrack courtesy of the buzz of tinnitus. So what's it gonna be, detective? the voice says finally, caressingly. Another pause, then a rustling sound from the pocket of the trench coat. The sky black moving smoke. Below, orange tongues lick, hiss and sizzle. Hundreds of miles.

I'd toss my baby into the fire if that'd stop it. Hushed silence. Come now. It's true. I'm tired. You don't think they're tired too? The soldier doesn't answer. Victory requires commitment, son. A two-hundred-yard sheet of mud spills down the hillside, pushing over houses and cars, wrapping around tree trunks, burying the unfortunate or careless or stubborn or anxious who remain to watch over their possessions, wiping them out in a thick, wet flow that scarcely burps consuming them, continuing on unabated. The pencil scribbles across the lined notebook page. So what, then, is required? Who is called to act? If humanity as a collective enterprise will not willingly pinch out its own buds, someone—some one of us—must step forward to do the deed. To do it and be hated and vilified, yet be heroic. To save the species from itself. To cull the unchecked growth and so bring the tree back into balance. I will be that pest, that super bug, that cutting sting that sets off the pandemic, reestablishing the sustainable future. Zip. Bang! Back on the bus, the woman sits as before knitting, occasionally looking out the window at the passing buildings and pedestrians. The strand of multicolored yarn—orange, yellow, brown, blue—slips up and around the needle tip then falls into line with those already set, continuing, stretching. Below is a five-inch strip of the stuff, folding and expanding as the woman's hands work above, lifting and lowering the whole with the action of the needles. A mess of worms slides one over another and over and around and under the scraps of sliced apple and dried leaves and carrot peelings and small mounds of spent coffee grounds. I am the composter too, the pencil scratches. The one who chews up garbage to cast it back out clean as fertilizer. The one who cuts down to restore. The pencil lifts and hovers. Lingers. I am the one who repeats. The 13-year-old girl sits in place, stiff, unmoving, her head slightly downcast and covered in the bright crimson wrap of her sari. Next to her sits a 56-year-old man in a white suit. The ceremony begins. Two men in dark uniforms rush into the crowd of immigration-reform protesters and take hold of a dark-skinned man. They ably wrestle him through the throngs of shouting bystanders and force him into the back of a white van parked nearby. Some of the protesters sit down in the street to block the van's path, but are quickly dispatched by police, and the van is allowed to pull away, driving twenty yards to the intersection, turning left and passing out of sight. The detective hustles along the street, his hands stuffed back into his pockets, which appear now to be filled with greater bulk—greater, certainly, than one would expect merely from hands. The detective continues to move quickly, swooping around light poles and the occasional, stray pedestrian without so much as a glance up. His head remains tilted downward, his eyes seemingly locked on the pavement in front of his feet, though the angle of this hat keeps his face from being seen. The boy turns the page. He lowers his mouth to his straw and slurps, generating a good deal of noise but failing to suck up more than a few drops of liquid from the bottom of the glass that holds only two small ice cubes. He shakes the glass with his right hand and tries again with the straw, having no more success. He grimaces and sits back up to continue his reading. The detective's right eye can be seen now peeking out from a patch of blackness. There is something sinister and yet fearful in the way the eye is drawn. In the next frame, with the detective visible roughly from mid-thigh up, he looks truly worried. Black lines of rain or shadow or streetlight slant down on him from the upper left corner. Next, he is glancing up and to his left, his mouth releasing a bubble of words that his eyes seem to be proofing. You gonna follow me the whole way? Then the bubble vanishes to reveal a ghost-like image of a black man's head, two or three times greater in size than the detective's, hovering over the detective's left shoulder. The phantom's skull is ringed by a thick afro, his lips and eyes evidencing mischievous glee. I'm right here with ya tec-tive, ha-ha, run the words printed below and slightly to the right (his left) of the spirit's chin, the sentence connected to his grinning mouth with a single black line. Be my guest, says the detective, seeming to shrug with a freshly drawn confidence. I've worked with uglier partners. Howls of laughter leap forth from the large ghost head, breaking loose of the frame to loop across the page in large, boldface font. We need to increase the birthrate in this country, the politician's face is saying, squared off by the edges of the TV screen. It's basic economics. We have an aging population that is retiring, and living longer than people lived in the past. Who's going to work and pay the taxes to support the entitlement programs that aid these people? How are we going to take care of our seniors? This is a serious problem. The situation is becoming unsustainable. And there's one answer to all this. We need to reverse this trend of decreasing birthrates. It's that simple. We need to bolster our population. Not through immigration. Not through handouts. But by giving birth to more children. More of our *own* children. The woman sets down her needles to answer her buzzing phone. Zup yo? she laughs, then remains smiling as she listens to the voice on the other end. She retains hints of the smile even as she begins to speak again. Right. Of course. No, yeah, of course we talked about it, but … She laughs again. Are you sure? smiling, though her lifted eyebrows betray some doubt. What do you mean you've done it? What have you done exactly? Her eyebrows pinch down and together as she listens, her smile fading, though her face maintains a hopeful, if moderated, air of expectation. She nods slowly, repeatedly, listening. When the farmer steps away from the barn wall—from his stage, as it were—she stands unmoving for several seconds, allowing the others around her to mill and circle, murmuring one to another as they take up their farming implements once again and head back to their chores or come together in small groups of three or four to discuss their leader's address or pass words of encouragement and assent amongst themselves. Then finally she lifts the wooden handle of the hoe that had been resting against her abdomen and meanders off, as if dazed by what has just transpired, lost in thought, directionless, apparently, allowing herself to be moved by a conditioned order that takes her out through an open door at the rear of the barn and leads her more or less in a straight line to the edge of the field where she had been working earlier and (as the blade of her tool lodges once again into the dirt) is now working still. God blessed them, saying to them, Be fruitful, multiply, fill the earth and subdue it, the farmer's voice somewhere crows. Be masters of the fish of the sea, the birds of heaven and all the living creatures that move on earth. Another drink, perhaps? Excellent! the disheveled businessman blows. Another drink for me and the lady! tossed off from already slurring lips to no one in particular—an imaginary barmaid, perhaps, whom he expects to be there, but isn't, presently. A fact he seems to recognize now, casting about bewildered eyes. The woman smiles at him and pats his forearm. I'll find someone, she says, and slides out of the booth. Smoke billows up in a widescreen stretch of choking blackness, tips of orange and yellow sway above the trees. In the foreground, a dark house, looking small beneath the encroaching flames despite the structure's obvious sprawl, looking already burnt, its exterior dead in the charcoal shadow of night or obscured daylight. Here we go, she smiles, sliding back into the booth and setting two pint glasses of stout on the table. Ha! the man caws, taking up the glass and quickly swallowing large gulps from it. The woman leaves her glass untouched and with a bemused look watches the man as he continues to drink. Occasionally he pauses to mutter non sequiturs or outright gibberish, before drinking again, looking wide-eyed at the wood back of the bench opposite him. When he has finished his glass, the woman slides the other one over to him, doing so with a dramatic flair that has her swooping her head and neck into the motion. He sits back, perplexed and looks at her. He looks at the full glass, then back at her. Laughter breaks out on his face. For meeee? he asks cupping the fingers of his right hand to his chest. She nods repeatedly. All for you, she says. He leans away, squinting his eyes at her and grinning. That's mighty kind of you, he pronounces from his slow, numbed mouth. She nods some more and pushes the glass into his hand. The water bursts over the floodwall, shoots into the street. Piles of leaves, branches, a mailbox, a tricycle are swept up in the surge and are pushed rapidly forward downstream. Turned so that her back faces outward from the booth, blocking from view the man next to her who is now passed out, she unzips his fly, brings the scrotum out from his boxers, then covers his genitals with a paper napkin. She reaches into her jacket and retrieves her tool pouch. She unties the pouch and takes the hemostat from it. Working quickly, expertly, she punctures the scrotum, tugs a cord free, clamps it, snips with a scissors, ties it off, returns the two ends to the sack, then draws the other cord out and repeats the process. She takes a Band-Aid from her pouch, unwraps it and pushes it on over the puncture wound. Her hand cups the scrotum and cradles it back into the boxers, zips the man back up. She returns her instruments to her pouch, reties the cords and slides the pouch back into her jacket, looking over her right shoulder to quickly scan the restaurant as she does so. Then she removes the man's wallet from his coat pocket, takes the cash from it, places one twenty-dollar bill on the table and stuffs the rest, perhaps fifty dollars in various denominations, into her jacket. She returns the wallet to his coat pocket, then takes a black marker from her own jacket and scrawls the following words upon the twenty-dollar bill: *No! Never! Really!* She recaps the marker, returns it to her pocket, takes a last look at the man, turns and slides out of the booth and exits to her right. The scientist drives her sedan down the ramp of the parking garage and pulls out into the light afternoon traffic. She drives slowly, chewing her bottom lip. A public radio news program is playing on the radio, relaying information about a shooting that occurred earlier in the day at a location not far from where the scientist is now driving. She looks to the radio and turns up the volume. Her eyebrows pinch together in the apparent effort of listening more closely to the broadcast. One person was dead from a single shot that investigators suspect might have come from the roof or window of one of the downtown buildings. The surrounding area has been blocked off and authorities are still performing sweeps of various buildings. They have not apprehended anyone, and police say they don't have any suspects yet, nor even a description of the shooter. They advise people to be vigilant and stay away from downtown if possible. The woman's hands flex at the top of the steering wheel and she rolls her shoulders up and back a few times. She puffs her cheeks and exhales. Infiltration, she says. He pushes himself up from the base of the trench, using his right hand to press back against the wall and aid his legs in lifting his weight. Upright, he starts off, threading his way through the long stretch of walled-in soldiers standing or sitting in the trench, alone or in small groups, silent or conversing, loudly, jovially or in soft, conspiratorial tones, acknowledging no one as he goes, nor being greeted by others, neither hurrying nor taking his time, a blank look on his face disguising his intentions, if, in fact, he has any beyond simply moving. The faucet handle is turned and the pipe coughs, spitting water from its mouth. It then goes dry and silent. Deep in the wall something moans, then knocks. The loud report of a shotgun, and a body falls. Indeed, Rebecca means almost nothing to me now, the man says into his phone, his shoulders relaxing from their formerly tensed position. You don't have to go that far, the woman on the bus says into her phone. I don't expect her to suddenly—or ever—mean nothing to you. But she does, the man insists. It's surprised me as well. But I lost it all, felt absolutely nothing walking back to the office earlier after seeing her at the café. The woman appears on the verge of responding, but remains quiet. She's completely extreme now, the man tells her. The woman nods. You can never tell, she says. The detective slides into the restaurant booth. He takes the passed-out man by the shoulders and straightens him up a bit, turns him slightly. Then he pats the man down from his chest to his waist. Finding nothing, at least nothing of interest, he takes the man's chin between the thumb and forefinger of his right hand and swivels the skull to the left and then to the right, inspecting the man's face. He puts the head back against the wood of the booth and allows the man's body to slump more deeply into the corner. As the detective makes to leave, he catches sight of the twenty-dollar bill lying on the table. Picking it up, he runs his thumb along the bottom of the bill, underscoring the words written there. *No! Never! Really!* He lays the bill back on the table and, while continuing to look at it, raises his hand to his mouth and traces the line of his lips with his thumb. Then he raises his hand to the brim of his hat, tugs it down, turns and exits the booth. The two-year-old girl wails into the phone that's being held to her ear by a soldier in green fatigues. Tears stream down her cheeks as her mouth gapes, her cries cutting off abruptly as she gasps for air. The murmur of a voice, female-sounding, bubbles from the phone's speaker, incomprehensible. An Excel spreadsheet is opened and a family name entered in the cell at the bottom of the first column. A first name is then entered in the adjoining cell, followed by the number 6 in the next cell, another last name in the next, a first name, the word "unknown," and finally an eight-digit number. Next! a voice calls. WHAT'S STOPPING YOU? the poster asks, the words printed in three-inch-high letters stylistically frayed at the edges as if applied by a paintbrush. Your Future Awaits …, printed in smaller, classical typeface, appears at the bottom of the poster, separated from the large, all-cap words at the top by the image of a young Asian woman in a dark navy suit with knee-length skirt, her face alight with a broad smile bordering on laughter, arms happily swinging as she sails along a city sidewalk. Her right arm, cast out in front of her, holds a slim, portfolio-like case that if she were to let go might be sent hurtling for quite a distance. Infiltration, the scientist says. The question is how, exactly? How did they get into the bloodstream? Was this an intentional invasion—an injection? Or was the subject infected in some manner without being aware? Is he or she still unaware? Is this a self-replicating organism or bot, even? A stealth virus or army of microscopic machines waiting to be triggered? And, if so, by whom? The shovel strikes the dirt, picks up a large load of it, casts it into a pile on the left, then returns to the earth for another load. Heat radiates off the hood of a parked car. She slips the noose around her neck and steps from the stool. Can you tell us if the reports are true? the reporter asks. Did you and your colleagues in the legislature, in your caucus, conspire to suppress the intelligence about these financial contributions? The man being addressed, probably in his late forties with a full head of expertly coifed dark hair and dressed in a well-tailored gray suit with a red tie, laughs upon hearing the question and leans back a bit at the waist. More stories, he scoffs. I don't know where you people get this stuff. Are you saying, then, that these stories are not true? she asks. Of course they're not, he replies glancing away, annoyed. Still, others are raising serious questions about the origin of these contributions and are calling for an investigation. Do you … *Serious*? These people aren't serious, he spits. He eyes the woman long and hard. They're no more serious than you are. They're just attention-seeking cunts like you. The reporter's head jolts back and her eyes widen, but she manages a nasally laugh. You realize you're being recorded, representative? I realize perfectly well, he says. And I stand by my statement. It's cunts like you, looking for trouble where there isn't any, trying to sensationalize everything, pathetically hoping to increase your ratings or clicks or likes or whatever it is—cunts like you who are preventing us from getting this country back on track. I'm just doing my job, the reporter tells him. Well, not anymore you're not. He draws a handgun from his jacket and shoots the woman twice in the chest. Infiltration, the sergeant opines. What else can you call it? The soldier in front of him nods. They're coming fast and furious. It's all we can do to corral them, get 'em hosed down and fed. And the stench … Don't get me started on the stench, the sergeant moans. It's burned into my nostrils. I taste those fuckers when I eat. The soldier chuckles. Everything I eat now is *Southwest*, the sergeant says. Like shit on bread. The soldier smiles and nods. That's it. Exactly. I smell 'em in my sleep. When you're not dreaming of banging their women, eh? the sergeant suggests, pointing a finger gun at his charge. No, sir, the soldier assures him, even that pussy tastes like shit, propelling his sergeant into howls of laughter. Next, the detective can be seen slipping through the opening of a barely ajar door—a trench-coated body and fedora-obscured head disappearing into a vertical stripe of black ink. The boy turns the page. Ain't this the shit, the detective says or thinks. How many times did I assure myself—promise myself—that I wouldn't hole up again within these walls? How many times? He sits down on a rickety wood chair in the corner, some stray light supplying (barely) the requisite illumination to make out the line where two walls come together and enough of the chair's scratched outline to identify it as a seat. The detective reaches inside his coat and draws out his kit. He unties it and lays it out on his lap. Then he reaches in the opposite side of his coat and grabs a baggie of black silt. He sets this on his lap with the rest, then sits up and pulls the coat off his left arm. Returning to the gear on his lap, he unseals the baggie's ziplock and takes a pinch of the silt. He deposits it on a spoon resting at an angle across his left thigh, then zips the baggie closed. He takes the spoon in his left hand and brings it up close to his lips. It jitters there awhile as he works his jaws, the tongue pressing back and forth against the upper row of teeth to produce a dose of saliva. He dips his chin and allows the spit to leak over his lips and drop onto the pile of silt in the spoon. That done, he lowers the spoon from his mouth (the effort required to keep the forearm, the wrist, the hand, the fingers steady and not explode in a palsied disaster is somehow evident in the hard lines that reveal the appendage) and mixes the silt and saliva with his right index finger, twirling it in slow, clockwise loops until the mixture has become a thick, black soup. He brings the finger to his mouth and sucks it clean. Then he grabs the lighter from his lap and flicks the flint with his right thumb to begin heating the spoon. When it starts to generate smoke he sets the spoon and lighter on his lap again and hurriedly takes up the rubber strap to tie off his left arm, spitting the words stupid motherfucker through clenched teeth, how could you forget … But having the strap tied on his arm now, he grabs his syringe and smoothly draws the warm silt bath into it. Taking the rubber strap up with his teeth and pulling it taut, he slips the needle into his arm and pushes the black fluid in. It's too late. The flames are just over the ridge now and the family must get moving. The man tosses a final bag into the back of the SUV and closes the hatch. He skips around to the driver-side door, which is already open, slips inside, closes the door and starts the engine. A wave of black smoke presses in against the windshield as he backs away from the house, then fully envelopes the vehicle as he shifts gears. But the smoke wisps away almost instantly, to the vocal amazement of the other passengers, as he drives forward onto the road, glancing for a time in the rearview mirror to check the progress of the fire. In one cell is written "Criminal history: burglary, drug possession, traffic violations." In the next: "Sterilize." She lays the cash on the counter and takes her coffee. She carries it out to a table in front of the café and sits there and drinks for a while, watching the two layers of traffic—human and machine—the closest moving (in a bidirectional weave) at a pace and rhythm concomitant with the heart; the other, beyond, rolling at a more liberated speed, as if on a stream of air, unrestricted by the limits of human function. Rebecca reaches inside her jacket and takes out her tool pouch. She sets it on the table, then reaches in the same pocket to retrieve her cigarettes. She slides a cigarette from the pack, places it between her lips, lights it. She removes it again, pinched between the first and middle fingers of her left hand, and blows smoke. A passerby catches wind of the floating nicotine cloud, turns and scowls. You're killing all of us, you know? Not quickly enough, Rebecca responds. The painting has the proportions of a 40-inch widescreen TV. Appearing slightly left of center is the bust of a man in conventional suit and tie, a TV news anchor, perhaps, though his forehead is tilted forward and his eyes are downcast and he is grimacing. His nose is crooked, maybe from a poorly healed break, and his forehead evidences a split down its center as if his skull had been bashed in at some point. Aside from the suit and tie, and the fact that he is sitting upright instead of lying face down in the dirt, the man bears a striking resemblance to the anguished figure in David Alfaro Siqueiros's *Postrado pero no vencido*. Behind him, on either side, stretches huge machine works, reminiscent of those in the social-realist paintings of Diego Rivera, complete with the teams of neatly aligned men and women in identical, romanticized, blue and gray clothing, putting shoulders to machinery levers, thick legs and forearms flexed and pumping. Yet here the levers they command are wholly useless, linked to crudely broken gears, cracked pipes leaking oil, and iron girders so thoroughly rusted that in some spots they have become a translucent orange. Where Rivera might have put the billowing steam of industrial might, here there is dark smoke rising from machinery on fire. The fires lead us away into dark tunnels and caves in which twisted scenes from Bosch or Bruegel play out: stricken gnomes, oversized bugs and dogs and other unidentifiable creatures gleefully engage in—or have fallen victim to—the most diabolical forms of torture, involving lances, chains and pulleys that pierce and contort bodies to the torturers' will. Moving farther out toward the edges of the painting, the Rivera figures return: stone-faced (or faceless) military and policemen in riot gear charging in on the painting's core in menacing rows, 21st century firearms at the ready. Beyond them, at the very edges of the painting, we see flames (upper left), rain and lightning (bottom left), crashing ocean waves (upper right), and baked, cracking desert (bottom right) that seem to lash the military forces into action. Following them in toward the center of the painting, the eye now picks up the fencing missed on first inspection, the chain links and razor wire cutting through the broken machinery, separating huddles of workers from their colleagues. Differences in flesh tone also become apparent now, with like-skinned workers fenced off from those of lighter or darker shades. Or is it just a difference in lighting between the different spaces that the workers occupy? Offset by the fence lines, the machinery itself takes on a different character, appearing more as walls or rock formations from which the workers are attempting to push their way through or over. The pained anchorman (or is he some kind of omniscient overlord?) is silent still and doesn't look. He left in a huff, Rebecca tells the other woman who has joined her at the café table. She punctuates the remark with a kind of nasal laugh. He would deny that characterization, of course, but that's how it was. Her companion nods several times. He doesn't like the vasectomies? Ha! To put it mildly. Again, he would deny that, but he wouldn't tell you he supports me, either. The other woman starts nodding again, but says nothing. He would agree that something needs to be done, agree that the abortion bans are a horrendous reassertion of patriarchal control. Weave nifty lines of Marxist-feminist political theory that spin on for hours seemingly. But is he willing to actually do anything about it? Anything that protects women or the planet? Anything to give a jolt to the assholes who are imposing these draconian measures, or to those who are happy to sit by and watch it all happen? Not so much. She takes a sip of her coffee and looks at the street. Her companion nods some more, but her look has turned sour. She leans back in her chair. Maybe he's seeing someone. Oh, ha, yes, I imagine he is at that, Rebecca says. She shrugs. It's just as well, really. Keeps him out of my hair. She takes a final drag from her cigarette and presses it out against the edge of the table. She sets the butt down next to her coffee, spending some time to adjust the alignment so that it's neatly parallel with the table edge. He won't turn you in, will he? Rebecca shakes her head, still playing with the cigarette butt. No, his timidity cuts both ways. He's not prepared to act—to *commit*—one way or another. I might actually regain some ounce of respect for him if he did snitch on me, she says, looking up finally from the cigarette and smiling at the other woman. If there's one thing I can't stand it's timidity. He's such a pussy, really, she laughs. She is humming, but then stops abruptly and stands up straight, relaxing the grip on the hoe. She wipes her forehead with the sleeve on her left forearm and exhales a defeated, all-this-exertion-is-pointless kind of exhalation, a what-am-I-doing-here kind of exhalation, and looks around to the others scattered about the field, rhythmically, mechanically working the dry earth with their tools, raking shallow troughs into the dirt. Neat parallel lines striping the entire field. She wraps her tiny fingers around the bar and seems to leverage it to pull her forehead forward, up against the cell's bars. And as soon as her soft toddler's forehead presses against the steel the tears come. Her mouth gapes, but releases no sound. The girl turns the page, her own face a bit rubbery now, struggling with emotion. Your mama didn't want you, the guard tells her. Told us to keep you. She walked right away, he says, shaking his head. But don't you worry, cutie, he adds, lifting a fat, weathered finger to her cheek, we're gonna take care of ya. OK? You'll be OK, ya hear? The girl cries loudly now with both hands squeezing the bars on either side of her soft, red face, her piercing scream cutting off only when she runs out of air and needs to suck some more in, choking on it, before returning to her wailing. The guard watches her for a while, then turns and walks away. A few drops hit the dirt, showing dark, wet circles that expand the slightest bit then begin to evaporate in the bright afternoon sun.

They come in musical clusters, dropping across the field as a sprinkling percussion, not at all constant, just frequent enough to occasionally offset the blazing heat. When the next batch comes, she lowers her head, catching some drops on the back of her neck. She lifts her hoe again and begins to work, casting the tool out in front of her and raking it back through the dirt, stepping back and repeating. The nozzle zips back and forth dispensing lines of blue molten plastic that cake one upon the last, fashioning, after a time, an upside-down L-shaped block, albeit one that slopes in at the top, causing it, on further reflection, to perhaps appear more like the head of a duck, the slope representing the dip from the duck's crown to its bill. And on that slope, or in it, rather, there is a large rectangular notch, a sort of compartment with cylindrical nubs jutting from either side that look to be fixtures for some other part that, presumably, will be printed separately. Be Alert! the handbill advises. It is lying at the center of one of the café's outside tables, its top right corner clamped by the weight of an abandoned white mug that still holds a swallow or two of coffee. The government is complicit in the racist reshaping of our country, the text continues. There has long been a corrosive network of reactionary elements operating within our government, its reach extending from the surface, the very public forums and chambers, down to the deepest, most secret parts of the governmental apparatus. And while its operation is opaque and complex, its objective is all too simple and clear: the eradication of the white race, our religion and our culture. BE ALERT! It will take the watchful eye and tireless efforts of all concerned citizens to unravel this dark cabal and restore our country to its former splendor. He is next to her now, his hand upon her upper back as she leans forward to work the earth. He leaves his hand in place until she straightens herself and turns toward him. Come to my quarters later, he says softly, his lips evidencing the beginnings of a smile. We can discuss your daughter. The chattering noise of the crowd encroaches on the stage like smoke, surrounding the lone microphone that's set up there on an old metal stand. Swirling lines of conversation interlace, with one or another gaining prominence for a time and rising above the others so that everyone in the crowd can hear and follow it for the few words of its supremacy, but then lose it again just as quickly as the words subside, dipping into a moment of relative silence or being replaced immediately by a new stream of words from another table. And so it goes for several more minutes until a spotlight suddenly illuminates the microphone onstage and the crowd noise lifts in unison then abruptly goes quiet. A man walks onstage from behind the curtain and stations himself behind the microphone. Thank you for waiting, he says, squinting out at the crowd. As you know we have a very special guest with us this evening. Samuel Bachos is the author of two novels, a short story collection, and a little book on the psychology of ants. His work has also appeared in the New York Times, The Paris Review, The Gettysburg Review, and Boulevard, among other publications. He is the recipient of a National Endowment for the Arts Literature Fellowship and was a PEN/Faulkner Award finalist. His latest novel—a graphic novel—is entitled *The Detective Cometh*, and he will be reading selections from that book tonight, along with some past work, I believe, yes? He looks offstage. Maybe not? he asks. He's shrugging over here, he tells the audience, laughing and lifting his right arm to indicate where Mr. Bachos, presumably, is waiting behind the curtain. Well, in any event, the man at the mic continues, turning back toward the audience, I'm sure it'll be a treat. So let me get off here and let Mr. Bachos get started. Ladies and gentleman, please welcome … Again his right arm extends and the author emerges from the wings, turning slightly toward the audience as he walks onstage, lifting his left hand (which holds his book) in a quick wave, before turning back to his host and extending his right hand for the customary shaking. Both men smile broadly as they shake hands and exchange a few words that can't be heard from those seated at the tables. Then the man who introduced the author walks offstage and Bachos is left alone there behind the microphone. He smiles and nods at the audience. Hello, he says. A few in the audience respond in kind. Bachos reaches into his sport jacket and draws out a pair of reading glasses. He unfolds the glasses and puts them on. He stuffs his hands into his coat pockets and leans back, allowing his shoulder blades to press up against the brick wall. What a disaster, he thinks. So much scum prowling the streets. Endless packs of vermin. The pimps, the whores, the dealers, the druggies, the small-time loan sharks, the gamblers, the busted. He takes the cigarette from his lips and blows smoke. The cops, the priests, the immigration squad, the government officials sailing over potholed streets in government-issued cars to plush, taxpayer-funded offices in thick, concrete-reinforced buildings. He moves the cigarette back to his mouth and inhales. And me, he says, or thinks, pausing for a moment to consider which is which. And me, am I any different? The worst of them all, probably. He looks down the street, visibly anxious. Disgusting, he spits. Then he goes quiet, watching the slow, steady streams of traffic and pedestrians coursing over the streets and sidewalks, forming, as it were, a single organism that beats with the pulse of an unknown heart. The energizing force. And the cancerous elements that look to undermine it all, whatever it be, bring it down and start anew. If there be a difference. The detective smokes and sinks heavily against the wall, allowing much of his body to go limp and, essentially, fold in on itself. Still slouchin, eh detective? Like a wet noodle. The large head of the Negro floats nearby, laughing. The detective grunts. Nothin left to say, huh? Maybe all that silt finally did you in, eh tective? The detective's face remains in shadow, silent. Cuz there be a difference, tective. That I can assure you. There be a difference. There're the forces of good and there're the forces of evil. They *are* distinct. But it's discerning the difference that's the trick. *That* be the trick. But are you up to it, detective? Do you know where to draw the lines and parse one from another? The black man looks down at the rumpled private investigator who has become even more self-absorbed, his trench coat now fairly wrapped about itself, his fedora sunk low over his face, so that he might well be said to be in a cocoon, the black man looks down and appears to pity him. Nooooo, he hums, shaking his head. You ain't discernin shit, are you detective? You're cooked, eh? There's a rustle in the crowd and someone shouts, Wake up! Bachos raises his head from his book and peers out at the crowd, a quizzical look on his face. His eyes shift from one side to the other, then he lowers them and begins to read again. The detective begins to slowly slide down the wall, a groan bubbling from his lips. Wake up! The land cracks, dried beyond relief. Waaaaake uuup! The man sprints, his tie wrapping around his left rib and fluttering out behind him. His head turns in the same direction now, exposing a face charged with acute terror, the eyes large and looking backward. The soles of his loafers smack loudly against the cement as he runs along the nighttime street, the way slanting downward and lit intermittently by streetlamps. The soles of his shoes smack loudly, rhythmically, against the cement and his heavy breathing fills the rest of the space with a whistling intensity. The patient remains feverish, sweating profusely over skin that's dried and cracked from years of exposure to chemicals and the sun with a few patches burned flat and scarred. I'm not sure there's anything more we can do, the doctor admits to the patient's partner. If we'd caught it and acted earlier … Silt owes its name not only to its black color and fine, granular texture, but also to its smack-in-the-head death trip that causes users to black out almost instantly. They emerge from this oblivion fairly quickly, however, entering a sort of dream state that is difficult, if not impossible, for users to distinguish from everyday lived experience (in fact, many claim this as the drug's allure). Unlike LSD, this alternate reality comes without wild coloring and intense feelings of contentment or searing panic. Instead, silt users remain rather detached from the scenes they encounter, moving through them like invisible, omniscient gods unaffected by these strange environments and their inhabitants. In fact, if any feeling can be attributed to the drug's use it is a sense of power and superiority over all other people. Some users even attest to travelling through time, with a subset of these indicating that they have communed with a past that was not their own. The drug's effect, however, ends as suddenly as it starts, ripping off like a blindfold, leaving users to confront the hollowness of an existence that but moments earlier had been beyond question, but that since—*now*—has been exposed as pure fiction. This transition can happen so swiftly, in fact, and with such intensity that some new users immediately resort to killing themselves, so great is the discombobulating terror generated by the loss of the drug's effect. This sensation also explains why users become so quickly and intensely addicted to silt (or to "loam," as its cheaper, cruder form is known), preferring not to spend much time in what they once knew as reality but to expediently return to that exalted dream state, designated by many of silt's acolytes as the "underworld." Yet, after just a few weeks of consistent use, many users become confused about which world is which and may begin referring to reality as the underworld and to the drug trip as the real world. Such can be the confusion that some users attempting to quit the drug do so with the understanding that it is the drug that is throwing them into everyday reality, keeping them, the "silk rakers" (as they are known), from that other world where they exist as gods. They can't understand why they insist on torturing themselves by taking this drug (shooting, snorting, vaping, eating) that robs them of their omniscience and invisibility, and that fills them with such ignorance and dread. Other people try to maintain a foothold in each life, and that's what screws them up. They don't want to choose between worlds, even though it's hurting them. They still try to hold on, as if letting go of one or the other will cheat them of something. It's an innate impulse, an animal instinct that has them clawing to get back or maintain a grip on that former life that was once so sure but is now slipping away, and they feel themselves sliding down the cliff, unable to hold on. It's scary being torn between the two. But you gotta choose. There ain't no other way. He was a doctor in his former life, in that other world. An abortionist! That horror of horrors, which, naturally forced him underground when the political winds turned heavy and dark, making his choice an easy one. His story wasn't hard to believe, such descents to addiction and depravity are all too common, really, even if people still feel compelled to express surprise, disgust and superiority. His being black made the shift even easier for people to swallow. They shook their heads, perhaps muttered a racial epithet or two, then moved on with their lives, feeling all the more empowered because of it. Thus, Dirt was born! The boy turns the page of his comic and lays it open, faceup on the café table. He sits back in his chair and looks absently at the upper reaches of a nearby tree, the leaves of which are just beginning to turn brown, with a few, on occasion, rattling loose in the wind and drifting down to the grass or pavement. She looks at him and asks, Why is it so small? You don't even have fuzz yet. He shrugs and tells her that's just the way it is. He says it doesn't matter. She gives a quick sort of laugh, then tells him to put his swimming trunks back on. Let's get back to the others, she says, already turned and ascending the path leading up and away from the lake through the trees, her rounded hips swaying smoothly to the working of her legs. A new breeze catches the pages of his comic book and begins flipping them left to right. His left hand juts forward from the edge of the table to settle the pages. He turns the pages back to where he had stopped reading, then he flips the book over and lays it down on its face. She stands awhile outside the wood door, her right palm resting against one of the door's crude planks, yellow light filling the gaps left by the door's poor construction. Then she pushes it in, gently, with the door seeming to swing open of its own accord and her hand merely following its path inward. The farmer is at his desk writing in a ledger, an oil lamp at the desk's corner just beyond the book's edge emitting a wavering light. He doesn't look up when the door opens but continues scratching away with his fountain pen, a look of pained concentration, one perhaps inscribed by the lamp's uncertain light, tormenting the lines of his face into dark watercolor strokes. At the end of a line in his ledger he abruptly sets his pen aside and looks up at the woman standing in the doorway. He brings his hands together in front of him on the desk, the fingers interlacing smoothly. He looks at her and his eyes soften. You've long struggled, he says in a gentle, reedy voice, his lips evidencing the beginnings of a smile. She stands looking back at him with tired eyes and says nothing. He unclasps his hands, bringing the left up to his chin, the right to his left biceps, where it nestles into the crook of the elbow resting on the desk. He leans forward.

I've thought on it, he tells her, playing absently with the clump of hairs below his lips. It will be difficult, perhaps impossible, but I will do what I can to help you free your child so she can join us here. His lips relax into their smile, but the woman remains silent, making no sign of appreciation or acknowledgement, even. You seem hesitant, he says after studying her for a time. Do you not want your daughter to join us? Of course I want to be with her, the woman says quietly, her head tilting downward. The farmer's brow pinches in, his smile broadens. What is it then? The woman shakes her head without lifting her chin. The farmer sits back in his chair and releases a happy sigh. The chair creaks. I won't press you, he says. I'll begin some inquiries, talk to some people I think can help, and we'll see where it goes. I know this whole ordeal can make you freeze up, not know what to do. But I think it will get easier for you once the ball's rolling and you just have to follow along. The woman makes a noise. Hm? the farmer prods. I assume so, she says, nodding. Yes, of course, he smiles. She nods some more, and then the two of them fall motionless and silent for a while. May I go, then? she asks, finally. Of course, he beams, leaning forward again. Get your rest. The weather should allow for a productive day tomorrow. The field is coming along nicely, no? It is, the woman says. She takes the phone away from her ear and taps her thumb against the screen to end the call. She rests the phone on the knitting bag on her lap and turns to look out the bus window at the city street passing by. Her face is reflected by the streaked glass, her visage floating over the façades of buildings, parked cars and moving pedestrians. Floating. Going. Gone, sir. The munitions will hit the road a mile in front of the hordes. The way should be completely impassable. The lieutenant nods his square chin. Scurrying rats, he sputters. I love it. I can't say I don't love it. I remember the first bomb, the doctor continues. Turned up in the mail, and just by dumb luck didn't go off. It sat there on the desk in my office staring up at me like some kind of Frankenstein lizard patched together from metal and plastic pipe. A sudden ringing pressed in on my ears. My head felt ready to erupt in flame. But then, nothing. The perceived lizard went inert. Mocking me with a future full of torment. How many more bombs? How many bullets through the heart? How many riotous fools filling the driveway and shouting spit into the faces of my staff and my patients? How many more government crackdowns and threats of criminalization? Finally, it just got to be too much. I went down. When I came up again, he took my face in his hands and smiled at me. You could be my Jane Birkin, he said to me. He said *what*? her friend laughs, nearly choking on the words. What does that even mean? Rebecca shrugs. He was quite a bit older. I guess he imagined himself as my Serge Gainsbourg. About as ugly, certainly. So what did you say to him? Nothing. What could I say? It's all too bizarre. Did he start singing to you? Thankfully, no. I put on my coat and was out of there. It was on the walk home that I started to develop my plan. Suck 'em off, knock 'em out, snip their balls. Moi non plus, she says clapping her hands together. You're awful, her friend coos, sipping her tea. No, it's not me, Rebecca insists. It's all the fools who think we can change things simply by voting and griping on social media. The cowards who don't want to get their hands dirty. I'm done playing. He lifts his eye from the scope and peers out over the rows of buildings that stretch to the horizon, their flat roofs forming steps that push up and down in an ever-shifting field of metal and concrete. He lowers his eye to the rifle's scope again and soon after begins to pop off imaginary rounds, his left arm jerking the barrel upward, his mouth sounding the soft explosions, one after another, felling imaginary targets. He lowers the rifle, then, and stands it on its butt, holding the barrel now in his right hand, his right knee on the concrete of the roof, his left up and with the left foot planted firmly on the roof. He continues to look out toward the horizon. This canvas is likewise proportioned like a widescreen TV. From a distance it presents as a rather appealing image, with several rose-red splashes set on a variable field of dark brown. Moving closer, it becomes clear that the red splashes are, in fact, meant to represent rose petals and that they are floating in a bath of chunky sewage. The painting is titled *Memories*. The white rectangle bobs up and down above the slowly moving mass of people as they make their way along the city street, hemmed in by the line of buildings on either side. There is a near constant, pulsating hum in the lower register that emanates from the crowd. At times it grows in volume and becomes distinguishable as a roughly orchestrated chant, but the words can never quite be made out. On the white, rectangular sign, #Pray4Us is written in large black characters. Occasionally the sign is thrust up and down, before returning to its calmer, more rhythmic bobbing. Sound from the crowd expands suddenly and echoes in the trench of buildings, creating a dissonant, forceful blur of vocal noise not unlike the crackle of a wildfire. A flag now lifts from the crowd (or comes now into view) and begins waving back and forth above the heads of the people moving forward. A crucifix, attached to the top of the flag's pole, catches orange light from the sun setting over the tops of the buildings and reflects it as a pulsating, on-off signal. Gunfire rips through the crowd, scattering people like blown leaves, leaping over or under tables, darting for doors (one leading to a storage room, one to a small closet, one to an office, one to a back exit where the swarm of fleeing people quickly clogs up), some jumping in place or standing still. One of the latter now receives a pair of bullets in the stomach, doubles over and collapses to the wood floor. The gunman comes forward, turning his rifle to the left and right and pinching off a flurry of bullets as he advances. He sees the crowd amassed at the back exit, swarming about itself. He fires into it. Squirming bodies fall, stacking on top of one another, ceasing to move. The vocal chaos, however, does not alter, neither rising nor falling, but maintaining a constant rumble that echoes off the shelves in the bookstore. A man tosses a metal chair through a window in the office. He grabs the young woman next to him by the waist and lifts her up to the window so she can climb through. He grips the shoe of another young man to hoist him through the window. Then he jumps up himself, planting his hands at the base of the window, launching with the strength of his triceps and lifting his right foot up to the windowsill to propel his body through the window and out into the dark night. His left palm slices across a jagged piece of glass as he goes out. Fire rages again, catching the wood paneling and setting it ablaze. Fingers of almost white flame lift to the ceiling and explore the copper tile, which reflects and so intensifies the light that distinct swirls of black smoke can be seen reaching up from the burning walls and floor to cloud the copper ceiling in wisps of feathery blackness. There's the constant crackling of burning wood and, every so often, a loud snap and, less frequently, a decisive break and the concussive sound of heavy, structural objects collapsing, followed by huge billows of smoke pushing into the room. As it clears, the detective's haggard face can be seen behind it, the half-smoked cigarette still hoisted a few inches from the lips, held between two severely dry fingers, the skin blanched white and cut by a network of thin red lines. The cigarette is brought back to the lips, which purse to receive it. The tip of the cigarette burns orange and releases a wisp of smoke before dimming again to a stub of scaly ash. The cigarette is removed from the lips, a stream of white smoke is blown. The smoke quickly overtakes the moving cigarette, broadening its scope, slowing and severing into numerous wispy tentacles that tumble over one another, morphing again in spots and generating new strands that become less and less opaque, expanding and separating and finally giving way altogether, vanishing before the face of the detective and the cigarette that is lowered out of view. Shit, the mouth says. It spews forth from the large cement pipe in a strong continuous stream and drops into the slowly churning pool of waste. There it swirls, mixing with the steamed milk that has been injected on its surface in the form of a winged creature—a phoenix or a moth, perhaps—and beginning to eat away at the image's extremities. She lifts the cup to her lips and drinks. Worse than that, she says, returning the cup to the table, I think I'm being followed now. The other woman at the table looks concerned, parts her lips as if to respond, but says nothing then, merely sits studying the face of her friend. By whom? she asks, finally. Rebecca shakes her head. No idea. It's a feeling more than anything. Who knows, maybe I'm just going crazy. But I continually sense that there's something—someone—always just behind me, lurking at the corner of my vision. A former victim, maybe, her companion offers. Victim? Rebecca inquires with a mix of incredulity and exasperation. They're not clients, exactly, are they? the woman asks. Rebecca reaches again for her latte, looking away from the woman and bringing the cup up to her lips. She drinks and returns the cup to the table. No, they're not clients, she says. She looks at the woman again. Still, they've signed up for it all the same, haven't they? The other woman frowns and her frame droops slightly in the chair. OK, she says. I don't mean to get into all that again. She sits up and back. But I'd like you to start worrying about the consequences, nonetheless. I am worried, Rebecca says. But if I let the worry stop me, then I'm just like everyone else who's pissed and terrified about the future, but too scared about their own safety to do anything about it. The way things are going, we're all gonna get it in the end, anyway. Her friend nods, but her show of agreement is rather unconvincing. It's one or the other, the scientist says aloud to herself. She switches out slides and puts her eyes back to the scope. Distinctly delineated creatures, red in color and shaped like tiny seeds with fat bottoms and pointy noses, swim in a swamp of fuzzier, white-yellowish, circular life forms. The sharp, seed-like creatures plow directly into groups of the mushier entities that have massed tightly together to form large, multicelled organisms. The seeds make quick work of these clouds, cutting through and scattering the individual cells in all directions, where they spin slowly for a while before coming to rest, their circular forms further muddied, deflated, sinking in on themselves in a sickly manner. With the cells now separated, the seeds take to attacking them individually, ramming the sides of a cell repeatedly until it loses its form altogether and dissolves like specks of pollen in the surrounding stew. The detective finishes his cigarette and stomps it out under the toe of his shoe. He jolts his shoulder blades up and off the wall and then begins walking, his shoulders hunched forward now and his hands stuffed into the pockets of his trench coat. There is hissing, and grumbling in the lower register. Where is this going? someone asks. Bachos looks up from his book and squints out at the audience. He looks to his right and then to his left, becoming visibly annoyed. Are you going to listen? he asks. There is more grumbling and a few whistles now. Are *you* going to listen? a man at the back of the room shouts. A disdainful grin is formed by the author's lips. I'm here to read, he says flatly. Whooooaa! several audience members howl, almost at once. Am I not here to read? the author asks. No! another man shouts, which has the immediate effect of silencing the rest of the audience, some of whom turn and utter low-volume rebukes of this naysayer, clearly perturbed that he is not on the same page as the rest of the protesters and, in fact, seems only to have been caught up in the general feeling of confrontation without understanding what any of it is about. The true agitators feel no compunction about calling out his ignorance and misguided excitability, if they do so in relatively hushed tones. I'm not here to read? the author asks, now sounding somewhat bemused. The crowd remains silent for several seconds, then a woman at a table to the author's right speaks up, explaining the audience's objection. You can read, but you have to understand the responsibility of your reading, she tells him. What you read matters. It has implications. And, a man on the other side of the room pipes up, you can't expect us to sit idly by while you spew misogynistic and racist nonsense. Exactly, the woman agrees, nodding, first in the direction of the speaker and then toward the author, who stands silent now behind the microphone, one eyebrow raised in a show of irritated disbelief. He begins to shake his head, and the wordless howls erupt again from the audience. Racist! someone shouts, rather halfheartedly. The author looks toward the voice and shakes his head more forcefully. You're an idiot, he says, the words sounding quiet and slippery, as if they'd escaped the author's mouth unwillfully. She trudges through the predawn darkness, her oversized boots crunching past the thin layer of frost to slop in the unfrozen mud beneath. Reaching the barn, she draws a ring of keys from her coat pocket, sorts through them by the meager light of the moon, then inserts one into the padlock on the barn door. She turns the key and the lock gives way with the body spinning free of the shackle that hangs on the matching iron loops set into the door and its frame. She lifts the lock from the loops and opens the door. As they kiss, he slides his right hand into the curved back pocket of her jeans. After this, there is little motion to their lips, or any other part of them, as they stand there next to the steps of the apartment building, pressed together, unmoving, as if suddenly frozen. The woman on the bus watches them for as long as she is able, even turning in her seat to look behind her out the window. The bus veers slightly to the left, following the street, and she finally loses sight of the couple. She remains turned in her seat for a while, nonetheless, blankly staring behind her out the window at the passing buildings, apparently lost in thought. He still doesn't say anything and her look of frustration morphs into one of annoyed acceptance. She turns from him. If you don't want to go, just tell me, she says, almost inaudibly. He enters the building and is immediately set upon by three or four men, who efficiently restrain him and drag him off to a back room, a hand cupping his mouth from behind. A saw cuts through an extended limb and it drops into the pile of ash. The forester then turns the saw to the next limb and quickly cuts through it, allowing it also to fall into the couple inches of ash that covers the landscape. After all the branches have been trimmed from the fallen tree, a gang of foresters hook a large chain around the trunk and with a thumbs-up and a call from one of the crew the tree is hauled away. God is a Warrior, it reads.

This is tenet number one in a list of five printed on a poster that hangs in a black plastic frame on the barn wall just above the collection of milking pails, which she bends over now, lifting one of the pails up by its thin metal handle and standing straight again. She stays there reading the list or, at least, looking at it. Tenet two: God, through His holy anointed leader, will designate the time for war. Three: Fight to win so we don't have to fight again. Four: Stay within the will of God; prayer maintains His Holy Army. Five (barely visible in the predawn light filtering through the cracks in the barn wall): Freedom is in the Lord—reject tyranny! The boy stares blankly forward as the two nurses attend to their various duties, one occasionally approaching him to stick a needle into an emaciated arm or to check his pulse. The boy says nothing. His chapped lips are parted slightly over his teeth, the lower lip pulsating to labored breaths. The sound of a jet overhead, and people skitter in the street. Los asesinos han sido detenidos, the text message reads. Aunque nada puede restaurar la vida de nuestro colega, podemos lograr algo de justicia para él. Lée más … The journalist's thumb hovers over the hyperlink on his smartphone. But there's more, she says. You're aware of the sex trafficking in massage parlors, no doubt. Her friend across the table nods. So what's to be done about it? Do we just leave it up to the powerful, old men calling the shots in law enforcement? The same powerful, old men who are driving—who are supporting—these sex crimes? No, she says, looking down at her coffee. It's up to us to take action. She looks to her friend again, who returns her gaze, and the two remain silent for a time. And what is this action? the friend inquires finally. I'm afraid to ask. Rebecca swipes a quick finger across the air between them, a mischievous grin taking her lips: Cas*tra*tion. He takes a final drag on his cigarette and spikes it into the turf, where it is ground out by the toe of his shoe. He leans in against the tree, holding onto it with both of his hands and peeking out from behind the trunk, spying the workers who have returned to the field and are busy now raking the dirt with their hoes. You want some more of that, bitch? That's what I said to her and I slapped her again for good measure, to leave a good sting on her cheek, you know? One she wouldn't too soon forget. Then I slapped her again because her face wanted it—was asking for it. Dirty bitch. I slapped her, then threw her down and left. The rain pelts the window. Starting like a barrage of a thousand needles, the water soon morphs into a solid sheet, attacking the glass in waves, rattling it in its track and rushing down, flooding onto the house's siding. The force increases now, the window throttled by deep, pounding blows. When the glass breaks, the rush of air and spray of water knock over the ficus plant, causing it to cough up a mound of dirt onto the carpet. Then the seed splits, replicating itself. I'm not sure I've seen anything like it, she says. His forearm lowers from its former position parallel to the floor. He turns his head and looks on astonished as his hand lowers to the counter. The fingers drum out a rhythmic gallop, each digit from index finger to pinky lifting and falling in succession, several times over. The man watches them go, his eyes widening and brow scrunching in a look of silent terror. Then the forearm lifts again, slowly, mechanically, craning up from the elbow until it is parallel once more with the floor. The hand spins at the wrist so that the thumb is now facing up. The man reaches over with his left hand and grabs the right wrist tightly, continuing to look on in horror. A capsule a day, the doctor says. Take it at night just before bed, as it can cause drowsiness and dizziness. Your urinary flow should begin to improve within a couple of days. The butterfly drops midflight and falls into the tall grass of the garden. Other insects buzz, then stop. The detective steps out from behind the tree. A hoe hits the dirt and rakes. A gun fires. The muscle below the prostate grips like a fist then relaxes. There's a loud trailing whistle, almost like a scream. A black flash across the sky, or is it a shadow, recalled in the mind's eye only after the missile has passed, diving into the earth. Black dirt explodes in a shower of a million clods, forced into the air, hanging a split second, arching, then falling heavily to crash against the ground and scatter into still smaller pieces—smaller bombs—shot out horizontally, nearly parallel to the surface of the earth. When all the dirt has fallen and resettled, lying in clumps and mounds and brush-like streaks across the grassy field and paved road, the crater can be seen clearly. Its epicenter is several yards off to the side of the road, although large chunks of pavement have, indeed, been dislodged and cast up, resting now at various broken angles. In addition to this, the road is heavily covered with loads of dirt and rocks. Still, it is not altogether impassable as the army had intended, and it might be cleared away even more with some concerted effort by the caravan of migrants approaching from the south who are now, perhaps, only a mile off in the distance. He steps out from behind the tree. He steps out from behind the tree and begins to walk toward the field spotted with workers. The tiny girl lies on her side, her mouth agape and her wide eyes staring blankly in their sunken sockets. An orderly removes the diaper from around the girl's waist, revealing a fully emaciated buttocks, the line of the back cutting straight down to the legs, perhaps even hollowing out a touch where the fat of the bottom should be. The girl lies still, inhaling slow, hard breaths. A knife thrust into the side of the abdomen and the man falls. He comes up beside the immigrant woman in the teal-gray slacks and coffee-colored shirt and says a few words. He draws a pen and journalist's notebook from his trench coat, flips the notebook open. He speaks a few more quiet words to the woman and jots something down. The woman, who ceased her tilling shortly after the detective approached, is standing upright now with the butt of her hoe leaning against her abdomen, her right, gloved hand keeping it from falling. She has an anxious look on her face as she listens to the man. Occasionally she nods or shakes her head, looking more anxious with each acknowledgement. Has he inquired about your daughter? he asks. Has he offered to help you with immigration? Are there religious obligations connected with your residence here? Anything sexual? He wants a child, I suspect, the woman says into her phone as she exits the bus. But he would never admit that, of course. In that way he remains beholden to his partner ... wife ... whatever she is, she laughs. She listens to the response on the other end of the line as she walks up a quiet city street populated by trees in nicely groomed concrete planters. No, the woman's crazy. There's no question about that. I think she's into some pretty nefarious shit. The woman turns at the corner and continues walking. I can't say for sure, but from some of the things Simon tells me, which are always quite vague, but, still, I get the sense that she's engaged in criminal pursuits. No—seriously! Her feminist activist shit is out of control. I mean, I agree with a lot of her positions, philosophically or whatever, but her means for achieving them ... I don't really know what she's up to. But I wouldn't be surprised to read about her in the paper someday. The woman stops speaking to listen to the person on the other end of the line. She groans. OK, she laughs, read about her *online* someday—you know what I mean. I wouldn't be surprised to learn that she's murdering people. Seriously! That bitch be messed up. She turns and walks up the steps of an apartment building, withdrawing a set of keys from her purse as she does so, the phone clamped between her ear and shoulder. I just hope she doesn't implicate Simon. He's too good-natured to know when to back off, get away. I don't know, I worry he's already too involved. He can be frustratingly naïve at times. Get off! The farmer, struggling to sprint across the field, his hips and shoulders rocking awkwardly to navigate the hills and valleys of dirt, advances toward the woman and the detective, his voice and right arm pushing into the wind, which robs each of its projecting force. Get off! This is private land. The woman fiddles with her hoe, rocking the handle back and forth in front of her, seemingly undecided if she should get back to work or hold her position. The detective hardly registers this turn of events, but stands casually watching the farmer advance, more annoyed by the disturbance than concerned, seemingly. This is *private* land, the farmer says, coming up. Indeed, the detective replies, and I am a private dick. The farmer is taken aback by the response, but quickly recoups his fury and takes hold of the woman's hoe. Raising the tool into an attack position and guiding the woman away with his left arm, he steps forward toward the detective. This is God's private land, he says. We don't welcome the devil's foul language, nor his foul scent. The detective doesn't budge. He glances down at his notebook. How 'bout devilish inquiries? The farmer steps forward with the hoe, causing the detective to finally take a few leisurely steps back. Smite not, lest ye be smitten, he grins. He reaches into his coat pocket and produces the pistol. Let's all be reasonable. The farmer scowls at the weapon, but relents, relaxing his shoulders and lowering the hoe to his waist. So we're two live spunks with our cocks out in the breeze, the detective observes. How 'bout we show the lady some respect, bury these tools away, and talk civil-like? There'll be no talking, the farmer says. It's time for you to leave. The detective looks now at the woman who has remained almost perfectly still throughout the encounter. I hope you won't hold any of this against the lady, he says, turning back to the farmer. She had nothing to do with me being here. I'm asking you to leave, the farmer says. The detective looks again at the woman, who lowers her head. He turns back to the farmer, studies his face for a moment, then nods and buries his gun away. He takes a few more steps back and looks about the field. Nice place you got here, Isaac. He smiles slightly as he turns to walk away. Real nice. He gives up and walks from the stage, still shaking his head, with some hoots and strings of condemning conversation accompanying his exit and continuing for a time after he has disappeared behind the curtain. Then the crowd falls in on itself and the noise of conversation spreads out, becoming a rumble of indistinguishable lines of talk, some propelled forward with an excitable rhythm in the higher register, some more subdued and low, supplying a steady undercurrent of bass noise. Unbelievable, the boy says. The girl stops reading and looks at him. What is? she asks. This, the boy tells her, laying out a hand, palm up, on the page of his comic book. This! He smacks the back of his hand against the page a few times for emphasis. It's all so crazy. Why would he just show up like this? Why would he go to the farm at all? I don't get it. The girl shakes her head. Don't ask me. It's your stupid book. When will we go? Rebecca asks. Simon gives her an uncertain look. What's wrong with staying? he asks. Smog lingers over the roadways like a heavy, multilayered pillow, choking the town on petroleum fumes. The iron rips apart and gallons upon gallons of dirty water gush forth. She holds his gaze for several moments, then spins from the table in a rush. The blood runs from the upper right of the canvas, flowing like a river to the bottom left. The source is a dark cave at the base of a mound of fleshy landscape, a pitchfork planted in its belly. The farmer remains there looking at her for a long while, saying nothing. She focuses on the dirt at her feet. We're so close, he says. We're so close. We can't give in now to those who would tear us apart. The kingdom is coming. The woman nods automatically. She moves the toe of her shoe in the dirt. Any word of my daughter? she asks quietly, the question sounding like a disturbance in the wind. A flash of anger, of impatience, before the farmer can check and resettle his emotions.

Not yet, he says finally, forcing a smile. But don't worry, the wheels are in motion. She'll be here. We just need to keep the faith. And before you know it, she'll be here playing on our knees. He hands the hoe back to the woman, smiling some more and patting her on the shoulder as he departs. The spotted bug lands on the broad green leaf and begins to chew. He spits onto the concrete roof. He lifts his rifle and peers through the scope. A thread of blue plastic wriggles just below the surface of the skin on his right forearm, causing the foremost end to poke free and shimmer in the sunlight. The wind catches the loose end now, tears it off, carries it away. It sticks into the left forearm and then the plunger is depressed, delivering the black silt. The detective inhales deeply, holds the breath, releases it. The gale continues unabated, pressing at the roofing shingles that flap back with the force. One rips off now and tumbles weightless across the gray, rain-sotted sky. Two, three, four more break loose and fly away. The roof begins to lift. The detective prowls through the clinic unseen, above it all, removed from the terrestrial goings-on. There is the woman, the one he will later come to know as Rebecca, in her mauve scrubs, guiding another woman into the examining room and shutting the door. There are the escorts briskly walking past, two of them, on their way back outside to usher in another woman, protecting her from the gauntlet of religious freaks. Here is Dirt, though surely he does not use that name at this juncture (if he uses it even now), in a white doctor's coat, a stethoscope stuffed into its pocket. He is engaged in conversation with a member of the clinic's staff, though the detective is unable to make out the words, the sound reaching his ears in a garble as if heard underwater or spoken through waxed paper. Yet both the doctor and the staffer maintain a relaxed, at times even jovial, demeanor as they converse. The staffer has a clipboard with papers, which she holds before the doctor and which he pauses now to read. He takes a pen from her and signs something on the page. The clipboard is then pulled back and held at the side of the staffer. The doctor says some final words and they both laugh. He turns and enters his office. The staff member passes by the detective and takes up her station again at the front desk. The detective stands still for a while, feeling the scene press in on him. Then he turns and follows the path of the woman who has returned to the front desk, walking—swimming—toward her as the front door opens and a man with a package enters. The tension is immediate. The woman at the front desk stands. There is a blur of voices that assaults the detective from all sides, motion that identifies itself as swirls of grainy color dissolving into space. The package deliverer attempts to pry open the top of the box as a handful of women descend on him. There is the extreme pressure of an anticipated blast. The detective sits under the tree, groggy, nodding compulsively, deep, guttural utterances bubbling from his mouth. Above his head on a limb somewhere there is a bird chirping. The sun is bright in the clear sky. The bird flies away. The brain is but a muscle, the rifleman says, the words evident in a bubble set next to his head and above the gun he aims at the viewer. And muscle shall splatter like a thousand seeds into the wind. They come upon the rubble, the mounds of dirt and rock, in a slow, cautious, curious line no more than three or four people wide at its broadest. BLAM! At the front of the group, men and women work, either alone or in teams, to clear the path as much as possible for those who follow. They are without tools, however, squatting and lifting large rocks and chunks of turf and lugging them out of the way by hand. The going is slow with longer pauses now between lifting and carrying and dropping a load and returning to get another, space filled with stretching of the lower back, hands on hips, the spine pressed up and bent back. Impatience begins to show on the faces of those in line immediately behind the removal crew, and some of these now step in to help, although with noticeably less commitment to the project, their loads less (typically only what one individual can lift on their own, and even that decidedly less than what could be considered a max load), the distance travelled to dump it less, their demeanors less restrained, showing clearly their perturbation. Behind these are those who have so wearied of the delay that they have begun to sidestep or negotiate the blockade as best they can, climbing over the rubble now and passing by the group at the front, trudging on without making eye contact. Some in the working group, caught mid-stretch, stand and watch these others go by, their initial looks of surprise, disgust, anger, annoyance making way for intentionally fierce visages of renewed determination (some) or dissolving into shows of resignation or relief (others) that split the group roughly into two halves: those who work now ever more diligently, likely overexerting themselves, and those who release a final, deep sigh, clap dirt from their hands, and join up with those moving forward. The brain receives the pulse and reacts. The subject turns his head to the left, his face adopts a pleasant demeanor, and he speaks. Yes, I can certainly do that, he says. Or he says, I give up. A pill bug skitters across the bottom of the bathtub, making its way to the drain. A spider drops along a brick wall. A robin sails in and perches on the railing. Rain pelts against the windows, resulting in a sheet of water that flows down the glass, obscuring the view to the outside, the cityscape reduced to vague smudges of gray, brown and green. You looking for someone, sweetie? Rebecca flutters her eyelashes and swings a sheet of hair over her right shoulder, combing it down with her hands onto her right breast. Someone to make you happy? Fire erupts in the dumpster, shooting flames up the brick wall. The spider hastily retreats. Moisture drips from the vibrating tailpipe, a haze of exhaust just visible against the neutral backdrop of the garage, choking the air. On the floor lies a woman, faceup, eyes closed, a trace of drool running from the corner of a slightly agape mouth down the left cheek. Step inside then, she says, responding to the man's quiet assent, her right arm extended, showing the way in through the spa's front door. Let me begin by offering the sincerest of apologies. If there is any explanation that I might offer it's that I was caught off guard in the moment and reacted in a noxious, defensive posture that only compounded the problem. Of course, I should have known better before that moment, before going onstage, so this is really no excuse at all. Obviously I need to step back for a while and reassess not only what I'm doing with my writing, what I'm hoping to accomplish and how I might be able to navigate it toward a more noble and purposeful literature, but also take a personal inventory and try to reclaim the nugget of decency and justice that I lost somewhere along the way. All I can ask (although I recognize that I'm in no position to insist on convenient treatment from those I've offended) is that I might be afforded the requisite space to perform this emotional labor. In return, I will commit myself to listening and learning so that I might, at some point in the future, be able to use my white, cis, heteronormative privilege in a way that will help lift marginalized persons and groups. Again, for what it's worth, I apologize to my readers, especially those in the audience that night that I confronted and offended, and I hope, with your help, that I will be able to work through this dark period and emerge on the other side as a force (if only a meager, striving one) for good. Yours in humility and struggle ... Cradling the nut sack in her left hand, she retrieves the scalpel from the inner pocket of her raincoat and with a quick, expertly placed slash at the top of the scrotum produces an opening from which she withdraws the right testicle. She cuts it free, then slices again on the other side of the scrotum, gaining access to the left testicle, which she likewise liberates. She places the extracted testicles into a Ziploc bag on the massage table, then zips the bag closed. She wipes the scalpel clean with a rag and returns both scalpel and rag to her coat pocket. From the inner pocket on the other side of the coat she takes out a prethreaded needle and begins to sew up the gashed scrotum. Hit the road right in front of them, you said. Make the road impassible, you said. The lieutenant gives a choked little laugh. Little punk, he coughs. You know what this means? The sergeant standing dutifully before him, stone-faced, his jaws registering just the slightest twitch of discomfort, of defeat, says nothing. Do you know? the lieutenant barks. It means you suck, that's what it means. And it means we're fucked. The hordes advance! the lieutenant proclaims, twisting his torso and casting his right arm skyward in a show of resignation. When they get here, I'll be sure to send them your way, sergeant. The lieutenant turns fully and stomps off. The sergeant remains standing there, alone, isolated. He lifts the cigarette to his lips and takes a long drag, burning the smoke almost to the filter. He rips the cigarette from his mouth and flicks it to the pavement, which is covered now by a sheet of gushing stormwater. The detective watches the surge carry the cigarette butt away. Then, as if just remembering that he too is situated there on the pavement, he lifts one foot then the other, kicking the water from each shoe. But, recognizing the futility of his situation, he sets each foot down again in the stream and makes a determined, if not overly rushed, exit to higher, drier ground across the street. The first drops of water hit the metal blade of her hoe and quickly run and mix in with the dirt she is moving. They come stronger now, pelting her hands and back and head. There is commotion suddenly about the field as sounds of hollering and movement complement the increasing pressure of the rain. Colors move about the field. She looks up and watches the others rush to collect their tools and streak across the field back to the barn, or rush to finish a particular stretch of their work even as the troughs fill up with water and their hoes furrow greater streams and toss muddy waves onto their shoes, ankles and pants. The woman has stopped working now, but hasn't moved to avoid the rain. Streams of water course down her hair and run over her clothes. She stands motionless watching the others. Her wet arms turn to gooseflesh. The bumps erupt, releasing noxious plumes of steam generated by the coal fire burning in seams beneath the road's surface. A deep fissure cuts across the road, casting one side of the pavement up, while the other falls sharply away. A row of green weeds lines the crack, filtering the steam. The gray, rotting corpse of a raccoon lies in the grass near the edge of the road, its mouth set open, its paws crooked into the air. A pair of flies circles above the animal's black eyes. A quick brushstroke adds a streak of rushing water. The head of a flower bobs in the late morning breeze, its pistil heavy with yellow pollen. A creature scurries through the underbrush. In the field still smoldering in spots from a forest-clearing fire, green tips of oil palm seedlings can be seen sprouting through the dark, almost black earth. The quantity and symmetry of the many green rows brings a meditative calm that clashes with the acrid scent of smoke and garbage that comes and goes with the wind. Several cracks from a rifle, and the orange fur of an orangutan can be seen shooting up through the branches of a tree at the edge of the forest. Water drips from the calved edge of blue ice. A creaking or moaning sound escapes from deeper within the landscape, the noise shimmering like the light upon the ice. Motherfucker won't be spawning no more fools, Rebecca pronounces as she lifts the elastic waist of the boxers back over the stitched scrotum. Pebbles shoot in against the glass as the rain comes hard now as if shot from a high-pressure hose. Wind rips at the roofing shingles. The parched, sunbaked dirt cracks and splits open. Ants run in and out in lines. A brown leaf tumbles across the arid crust, catching up finally in the hard, skeletal remains of a withered thorn plant. A kangaroo rat hops across the white dirt, disappears suddenly into a slight opening. Patches of blue plastic speckle the dark gray rocks on the shore. Having been pressed into the rock by the tide, the plastic now acts like a permanent, protective coating. The latest wave crashes against the shore, leaving a fizzle of foam when it retreats. Fire takes the house, crumbling to char. Black smoke clouds the landscape. Meltwater from the glacier delivers white silt into the fjord. There it hangs suspended, filling the previously clear water with swirling particles of paint. The brush is lifted out and scraped against the side of the jar. It is then directed to the palette where it is dabbed into a small mound of yellow paint. The kernels of corn are distinctly separated from one another by dark brown, almost black lines. Each kernel is outlined in brown, showing a bright, lively yellow only at its center, the overall effect being one of death and decay, the withering brown husks falling back and away. Black sediment is heated in the spoon. Stormwater rushes over the field, churning it to dark sludge. A crowd of people waiting outside the concert is sprayed with a barrage of bullets. The claret fetched flies. Bodies tumble. The detective grabs Simon by the arm, says, Listen here. Flies burrow into the dead animal's ear. We know everything she's up to. In the blow of sideways rain the tree snaps and falls. We know everything she's up to, the detective says. Maybe you better come with us. But you're alone, Simon observes, allowing himself to be guided along nonetheless. One step off the roof of the building and the body begins its eleven-story plunge. Automobiles clog into the chutes of the merging highways. Cattle are prodded up the ramps. Hail pellets drop from the sky in a mess of white lines, gather precipitously on the city streets. Seawater crashes over the embankment and floods onto the plaza, sending gulls skyward and soaking wingtips and cuffs of slacks. I have something important to tell him, but I can't bring myself to do it. For so many reasons. I don't think Simon will take it well. Rain continues to pound the roof of the barn, releasing a torrent of sound and threaded sheets of water that flow down and run off the roof's edge. Grouped inside around their leader, the adherents of farmer Isaac shuffle about, chattering to one another and attempting with towels or hands to wipe the water from their clothing. Isaac, standing as a dot at the center of the surrounding crescent of people, remains quiet, watching his flock with a troubled look. The group becomes steadily subdued, lowering their voices and, eventually, quitting their talk altogether as they pick up on the demeanor of their master and come into submission. Isaac gives them a weak smile. Have we dried? he asks in a friendly manner. There are some grumbled acknowledgments and dissents, some laughs. Isaac smiles more broadly and nods back at them. Good, he says, good. He brings his hands together in front of his chest and scans the group once again, relinquishing the smile. I'm afraid it's begun, he tells them, nodding once more. The forces of evil are gathering, closing in. He pauses for a moment, his gaze falling on the Indigenous farmhand who earlier had had the run-in with the detective. This has pushed our schedule, he continues, looking about the group again. I was hoping we would have more time to prepare, but if we are to emerge victorious—to claim victory for our Lord—then we must begin to execute our plan immediately. Shuffling returns to the group, accompanied by some murmuring. I'll be meeting with each of you, individually and within your mission groups. There is an urgency now—I don't doubt that all of you have felt it as much as I have. The Lord is calling us to act. Yet we must not become overanxious and undisciplined. We know our cause is just. We know we have been called to it. We know that our victory is preordained. Now we simply need to trust in it, allow ourselves to fall into our action and serve as we have been commanded. If we do this, all will end well. All will be completed. Flames take the trees, pushed along by the wind. Shots crack from the top of the building, picking off random pedestrians on the street. They fall where they are hit, soundless. The rifle reloads. The fan spins above the head of the man dozing in the wicker chair, his arms laid out on the armrests, palms up, deep red slits cut lengthwise into the wrists. The bodies, laid out so close as to be nearly piled on top of one another, can be seen to move occasionally, squirming this way or that in an attempt to gain a more comfortable position. A tart stench of bodies permeates the cage area, waxing and waning with the exhalation of breath and other emissions, the opening of crevices, the removal of shoes and other articles of clothing. But perhaps those lying there, who have been housed within the cage for weeks, no longer register the smell. She approaches the farmer as the group disperses, heading to their quarters or to various indoor chores. She approaches him and asks quietly, haltingly, How will this affect things? He smiles warmly on her, eyebrows raised, seeming not to understand the question. With my daughter, she says. His hand moves to her back. He frowns pleasantly. We'll see, he tells her. We'll see, but, yes, this quickening of our plans may disrupt things in that respect. Her eyes plead with him. He moves closer, turning to face her directly and taking both of her shoulders in his hands. Sacrifices must be made all around, he says. Hopefully she'll be able to join us. But if not now, you will be reunited with her in the not-distant future. The Lord will see to it. He will provide. The woman looks down and nods weakly. He takes a hand from her shoulder and uses it to lift her chin. He will provide. I'm bored, the girl tells the boy sitting next to her at the café table. When's Mom coming? He shrugs, goes back to his reading. The girl turns away from him and looks out at the street, which is filling up now with noise and traffic. Insects rage, commandeering trees and bushes, covering screen windows, infiltrating the hair on the heads of small children. Tinder crinkles in the ashes, flashing orange. Smoke drifts. I'm not sure what he'll want. I could see it going either way. Flames occasionally reignite from the beams of wood and just as quickly die away. The detective sits Simon down at the wood table and offers him a cigarette, which he declines. Should we begin then? Simon spreads his hands. As you wish. The detective shakes a cigarette from his pack, sticks it between his lips and lights it. He inhales deeply, pinches the cigarette between index and middle fingers, removes it from his lips, blows, points the lit end of the smoke at Simon. I've seen it all, he says. What have you seen? How she's trapped them, lured them into her lair. How she excited them, drugged them, knocked them out. How she cut them open and sterilized them. How she sewed them back up all nice like. All that back-alley stuff. The NNR Post-it notes. I have a fine collection of them in my office. Simon stares at him blankly, says nothing. Perhaps you could begin by telling me what these notes mean? No to reproduction, to be sure. But with what aim? Saving women from being impregnated? Reducing the human population? Surely she can't believe that she can achieve that on her own. Are her victims specially selected, then? Are these men who have wronged her? I don't know anything about this, Simon says finally. The detective shakes his head, flicks the ash from his cigarette into the ashtray. Oh, I think you do, Simon (he gives it a French pronunciation: see-MOHN). You know far more than you are letting on. Simon says nothing. We can sit here all day, the detective tells him. A drop of water falls from the ceiling and lands on the table between them. The detective looks up, watches another drop fall. The boy at the café table jerks back noticing the drop that has plopped into the middle of the right-hand page of his comic book and is now slowly, steadily expanding. He looks at his sister next to him, just as she feels a raindrop hit her nose. The gunner on the rooftop dips his left hand into his duffel bag and wrestles out a ball cap, fitting it onto his head to shield himself from the intermittent drizzle. Withdrawing the knitting from her bag to set it on the coffee table, Simon's ladylove looks to the window suddenly, startled by the quick rattle of hard raindrops on the glass. Businessmen and women on the sidewalk—heading to their cars, to a train or bus, or to a restaurant or bar—scurry under awnings or hug close to buildings hoping to avoid the worst of the lines of water falling from the sky. The detective puts his cigarette out in the large puddle on the table. He tugs down the brim of his fedora. The drip-drip will get to you, he assures Simon. Let's have the truth before you go crazy and start yelling absurdities just to gain your freedom. I've told you everything, Simon says. You've told me nothing! the detective growls. Exactly. The thawed peat crackles to life, ignites, releases its carbon into the atmosphere. A punch of wind shoots glass in through the curtains to litter the carpet. It happened about the same time I suffered the dent in my skull, he tells the man seated next to him at the bar. After that, slowly, my brain started to go a bit fuzzy. My vision changed, my ears started to ring, and I always felt congested. It became hard to think, and to *keep* thoughts, you know what I mean? The man next to him grunts and gives a single nod that leads him conveniently closer to his rising beer. He takes his drink, then tells the first man, You think that's bad, I suspect someone has completely taken over my body. The first man is skeptical, shows it on his face. How do you mean? I mean they've gotten inside me. Don't ask me how exactly, but they're in there, just the same, and they have control of me now. This seems to assuage the doubt of the other, who nods several times. And who's *they*, exactly? I don't exactly know, the other man grins. But I can feel them inside me, controlling my movements. Not so much my thoughts—not yet—but my movements, to be sure, as if they implanted tiny machines in my bloodstream. The other man is suspicious again. Maybe it's your thinking, in fact, that's all wrong, he suggests. You'll excuse me for asking, but have you considered visiting a mental health professional? There's a bit of a twitch around the other man's eyes. No, he says finally. No, I haven't. Maybe I should, he says, returning to his beer. Both men are quiet then for a spell, looking straight into the shelves of bottles on the other side of the bar and occasionally taking drinks from their beers. Maybe I should, the man repeats. But I have long dreamed of living in a world transformed by war or some other travesty. A world turned to chaos where past sins would be erased and the possibilities would be endless. The romance of living life at a level near starvation, surrounded by people who no longer feel the burden of moral constraints, where the ground could open suddenly beneath you, or a building or some other thundering object could come tumbling down on you … You could be anything you wanted in an environment like that. The man next to him hunches closer to the bar, considering the remarks. I guess you're right, he says, nearly inaudibly. It's time, as I've continually impressed upon all of you in the past, as all our time here together has been preparing us, to simplify. To simplify not only our mode of living, but, as we head into battle, to simplify our very beings—to simplify *spiritually*. Several of the farmhands gathered about Isaac nod in agreement, though the expressions on their faces betray less certainty. The mosquito lands, pricks, and sucks. The valve on the water spigot is turned, causing the pipe to choke and cough. Nothing. So you're really gonna play it that way, huh? Not gonna say anything? I'll tell you again, I *have* nothing to say. I know nothing. None of us knows anything, the scientist sighs to her colleague. At least that's how I'm beginning to feel. Things are moving too fast. What *is* this? she exclaims, extending a flat palm toward the microscope on the table between them. How can this even be possible? We've long theorized, her colleague attempts. Yes, sure, yes, I know. But we had no idea it was this far along. What else have we missed? They're forcing me to shoot people, the man at the bar says, before taking a sip of his beer. I can't say, though, that I really dislike it. Now clear of the rubble, the migrants continue their trek along the road, moving in clumps of five or eight or ten, some groups chattering, laughing even, some silent, their faces showing the effort it takes to continue walking, some occasionally breaking out in song, protest anthems or religious hymns meant to lift their spirits, apparently, the tunes winning over groups behind or in front of them for a time, raising the communal volume, before succumbing to the pressures of physical exertion and mental anguish. The line makes its way slowly toward the bottom of the screen, expanding and contracting with the bustling of individual members of the group. But before it reaches the limits of the monitor, the surveillance drone drifts back, reorienting the line of migrants so that the front of the group appears once again at the top of the screen. The needle is stuck in, the plunger depressed. Water floods along the ice sheet, a large chunk breaks off. An interfaith vigil for immigrants, the sign reads. Come join us in prayer and song each month at the federal building. Prophetic witness will stem the flow of hate and abuse of power! The farmer thrusts his pitchfork skyward. The Lord will prevail! he thunders. The rain starts. You will not replace us! the crowd chants. Fire takes the tree and sets it ablaze. The white-clad men kneeling on mats, their number filling up the room in tight rows, all bow forward. The parched dirt cracks. The knife plunges into the back of the neck. Bullets fly. The rain-loaded winds whip through the city, tearing at buildings and trees. Sweat runs down his temple, the heat being immense. They are like dogs, the monk wrapped in an orange cloak tells the crowd stuffed into a low-ceilinged room, breeding to overtake us. They hypnotize our women, steal them, rape them. The brittle, drying husks rustle in the breeze. God sees the evil we perpetrate, the evil we condone, the rotund preacher in a three-piece suit proclaims, wiping his brow with a white handkerchief. Homosexuality. Abortion. He sees it and he erupts. He does not weep, he erupts! Snow builds inch by inch, the fury of the storm turning the gray sky to static. This is a safety measure, the Indian official with neatly trimmed white beard opines. We must reach out, embrace and protect our own. It is about freedom. Nothing then? Nothing, Simon confirms. The detective stares at him for a strong moment, grunts and turns away. He jolts up from his chair, knocking it to the floor. Go on and get outta here, then, he barks, pulling the door open brusquely, giving passage from the small room. Simon gets up and walks unhurriedly out, eyeing the detective as he goes. The waves tower and crash. Seawater breaks over the wall. Gulls lift and cry. Rebecca presses the severed testicles, one after the other, into the mouth of the bottle. She shakes them down the neck till they plunk deadly to the bottom. She rolls the scrap of paper upon which she has written the words *No! Never! Really!* and inserts it into the bottle, whereupon, dropping into the body, it unravels, revealing the words again fully. She screws the cap on the bottle, grabs it by the neck, lifts it overhead and back, then comes forward with it and lets it sail, flipping out over the raging waters. It's humiliating what we must go through just to get the prescription we need. Treating us like common addicts. And for what? What does it solve? Nothing. Only brands us addicts to make the powers that be feel like they're doing something. #PrayForAmazonas. Seated cross-legged, then, on the beach, her hands resting with palms up on her thighs, index fingers curled back making loops with the thumbs, raising tendons at the wrists that are just beginning to cover over with leaking blood, she extends her spine, lifting up, closes her eyes. She hums in harmony with the roiling sea. The mouth of the universe opens its furrowed lips. (Or does it?) The temperature plummets. He tugs the cap down further on his head, levels the gun, fires. Boars, armadillos, snakes flee en masse from the forest now engulfed in flames. Thick smoke chokes the rescue efforts of those rushing in to quell the blaze. Winds whip and lift houses. It's raining again. She looks out the window that's flooding over with water. The detective steps out into the broad daylight, squints, lowers his head, lights a cigarette. Inhaling the smoke, he tugs the cigarette from his lips and looks up into the glaring sun.

He releases the smoke with a growl, squints into the sun awhile longer, then averts his gaze and begins to walk. The earth explodes, spewing loads of dirt and rock up, over and down onto the huddling soldiers in the trench. The crease cuts from the lower left corner of the canvas to the upper right, dividing the gray gravy wasteland of the battlefield from the darker, almost black, dirt of the trench wall. The huddled bodies tucked in close at the bottom of the wall wear gray uniforms that betray just the slightest hint of their original green color. The girl gets up from her seat at the café table and walks over to the street curb. There she squats to pet a stray kitten that mews up at her hungrily. There, there, she tells the kitten, as the U of her hand strokes the creature's thin frame. The boy at the table looks up from his comic book and watches her for a while, his face showing a quick succession of emotions from curiosity to worry to annoyance. It's probably diseased, he tells her. The girl shoots him an angry look and returns to her petting. The boy continues to watch her in silence. I'll tell Mom, he says finally. Simon walks the street alone. Rebecca's body, set in a position of pranayama on the beach with bleeding wrists, erupts suddenly in flames. Incense drifts. Dirt? You there, Dirt? The detective, inked with hands stuffed deeply in trench coat pockets, fedora tipped, obscuring face, lines of smoke swirling up and around the brim, walks a dark page. Dirt? Nothing. Isaac out front now leading his disciples through the night, all bearing torches that cast hard-lined, flickering shadows. Lorrrrd, we have travelled. Taken from our hooooomeland. Taken from our couuuntry. Taaaaken from our chiiildren. Ohhh-ohhh Lorrr-orrd. Leeead us home, Lorrr-orrd. The grasshopper inches up the thick blade of field grass, its forward limbs scratch at its face. A drop of rainwater runs the length of the leaf, then hangs at the pointed tip, reflecting light from the sun. One day at a time they say, Dirt. One day at a time. But if it's one day at a time why do they reward you for thirty days? Three hundred sixty-five days? Shouldn't one day be as important, or as meaningless, as another? All that this counting of days does is instill the foreboding sense of *forever*. And if you slip up and take a hit, it's back to the beginning, like Chutes and Ladders. Shame and guilt. The very things that drive you to the oblivion of drug relief in the first place. The anxiety-free who skate through life, what do they know about existence, Dirt? What do they know—what *can* they know—about the coming oblivion? They reject the very idea of it. Not like you and me, Dirt. But am I any better? Hunting down drug dealers, abortionists, contraceptionists, vasectomists, illegal immigrants, protesters, prophets, renewable energy advocates and users ... all for the price of their hides? And even as I, myself, use? Hooked on the silt, to the earth dust, just like you, Dirt. No better. Not a stitch better. Brothers in obscurity and disgust. The boy flips the page, traces with index finger the opening at the end of the gun's barrel.

One full circle. Taps his finger on the black center of the white barrel that is framed by black ink in the upper left-hand corner of the left-hand page, the barrel already yellowing, browning, decaying. There's but one solution, the detective says now to no one in particular. The girl returns to the table, carrying the kitten. She sits down, resting the kitten on her lap, petting it as it continues to mew—single weak pleadings in the upper register, separated by fairly uniform gaps of silence. She scratches the head now and the kitten pushes up against her fingers. Then she returns to long, slow strokes along the kitten's body, calming its demeanor, the mewing becoming more sporadic, its eyes growing heavy, its front paws kneading her thigh. The kitten drops now, purring loudly, rests its chin on outstretched limbs, slumbers. The girl continues to pet it slowly, gently, a soft smile warming her cheeks. After a while she quits the petting and simply watches the kitten sleep. Later still, with the kitten still audibly purring on her lap, she turns back to her book, flipping it open flat on the table and beginning to read again. With wind gusts approaching 200 miles an hour, the hurricane blows inland, tossing waves of water from the sea, battering homes and other buildings, destroying docks. Cars tumble in the wind, are lifted by rushing waters and float down city streets. Isaac and his troops come forward, their torches blazing at dusk. The detective peeks out from the corner of the building, his pistol at the ready. The book is nearing its conclusion now. Scenes become contrived, the plot rushes to a finish. The blackened skeleton smolders on the beach where once an old tire washed ashore carrying a castaway. Simon walks along a sidewalk, tapping on his phone, head down, negotiating the after-work traffic. His paramour receives the text, reads it and laughs. Isaac continues to lead his charges up the street. The detective's pistol shakes. One last deed, he mutters into the building's bricks. He steps forth. The two-year-old immigrant child, formerly held by the authorities, has been released and is currently en route to the farm (with the aid of a nonprofit immigrant rights organization) to be reunited with her mother. Her mother is on the street, roughly halfway back in the swarm of farmhands following Isaac. The glint from the blade of her hoe can be seen as it is pitched upwards, catching light from surrounding torches or streetlights. He spies the passing tire just in time and with outstretched right arm takes hold of it, releasing his left-hand grip on the gutter of a submerged house and swinging his body over onto the tire. Hardly has he established equilibrium on the tire, with his torso planted firmly within the circle of the tube, both arms clinging to the outer wall, than a new tidal wave rushes in, lifting him and the tire up smoothly and carrying them forward with terrifying speed. He rides out over the tops of buildings, bearing the brunt of lashing rain, flying rodents, and large pieces of wood and other debris shooting through the air. He buries his forehead into the tire's rubber, flexes his arms more tightly around the outer walls. Alone in his dark office, with only a gooseneck desk lamp illuminating the work he is doing with his hands, the doctor pours several pills into the mortar, then takes up the pestle and begins to grind. Once he has a fine white powder, he transfers it to a test tube, which already holds a finger or two of black liquid. He swirls the mixture by cycling his wrist, then grabs hold of the tube with a pair of tongs. He drags a Bunsen burner into the light from the corner of his desk. Still holding the tube with the tongs in his left hand, he reaches into the desk drawer with his right and pulls out a lighter. He opens the gas on the burner, clicks the lighter, gets a flame from the burner, adjusts its strength. He holds the tube at an angle over the flame. Soon the liquid begins to smoke and the doctor moves the tube up and back across the tip of the flame. Once most of the liquid has burned off, he extinguishes the flame and sets the tube in a stand on his desk to cool. He sits back in his chair and waits. The fan blades twirl in the window. On the bed, a man clothed only in boxer shorts lies sweating. He curls a magazine in his right fist, exposing a single column of text for reading. He bubbles an exasperated, exhausted exhalation from his lips, widens his eyes, then allows the lips to droop again as he tries to continue reading. The soldiers rise from the pit, slant rifles over the edge, steady themselves and fire. Gray clouds of smoke rush in against them. Corpses rot yards from their noses, flesh liquefying with earth in the rain. Worms and vermin slink through the mud. The soldiers fire. They duck and fall back. They rise again. Fire. The air a continual drumming of carbine and mortar blasts. Riding out over the tops of buildings that are sinking beneath the waves. He lets himself be carried. His wife, his two daughters lost to him now in an instant. Christ paid the ultimate price for it. Being robbed while unconscious. And a laugh. Out of sight. Fill the earth and subdue it. Moving. She places the slide under the scope, lowers her eye to the eyepiece. She inspects the slide's culture for a while, expressionless, then sits back finally in her chair and stares blankly at the wall on the other side of the room. He takes aim from the top of the building and fires. Fires again. Quickly, he packs away the rifle, slings it on his back, rises and heads for the stairs. The wound in the tree bubbles with a yellow syrup. Scores of ants trace the gash's outer rim. A cloud of gnats hovers. Talk to some people I think can help. Planted roughly halfway up the side of the trench. Lifting with his voice. The sleeve on her left forearm. Evidences a split down its center as if his skull had been bashed in at some point. The knife slashes. Tear gas funnels down the narrow city street sparking a mad dash of people streaking in colored lines to escape the noxious cloud. Shouts echo off walls. Sirens blare. Diminish and blare. In a cycle. Out at sea, he drifts, carried by waves. The detective steps out from behind the building and fires. Cockroaches scurry. Bad, you understand? Customary shaking. The street. Briefly then puts the erect penis back in her mouth. It's ending. The farmer takes the bullet in the left arm and grimaces. Hit suddenly by the nausea, she rushes to the toilet. Bent over, vomiting. Another round of shelling and the migrants fall, chanting prayers. Showing dark, wet circles that expand the slightest bit then begin to evaporate in the bright afternoon sun. Lick, hiss and sizzle. Effort of listening more closely to the broadcast. The tire washes ashore, the man falls off and becomes Isaac. The seventeen-year-old girl trudges north, carrying her two-year-old daughter. The doctor quits his practice, goes underground and begins dealing. The detective is a mess. He steps forward, takes a brick to the head and fires. Get in the car! their mother yells from the idling Subaru, it's late! Ashes blow across the sand. He drags a large duffel bag to him. Explosions, one after another. The hoe hits the dirt and rakes. The command is given. He fires. The farmer doubles over. The woman gasps. Simon meanders up the path, through the stone gate at the park's entrance, past the line of trees, round bends, and over small bridges. He sits down on a bench. The phone in his pocket begins to vibrate. Is diverted by a man passing by her suddenly on the left. Puts the phone to his ear and listens. So, she says, this shit's really happening. A bird caws. A fire burns. How so? he asks. You see, she begins, I'm pregnant.

About the Author

MATT MARSHALL is the author of the novels *The Starlight Line* and *Friction.* His short fiction and arts criticism have appeared in Guide To Kulchur Creative Journal, Muse, La Petite Zine, All About Jazz, Jazz Inside Magazine, Cleveland Scene, and Free Inquiry, among other publications. He lives in Cleveland Heights, Ohio.

mattmarshallwriter.com